The
Night I Met
Father
Christmas

The
Night I Met
Father
Christmas

Ben Miller

with illustrations by Daniela Jaglenka Terrazzini

SIMON & SCHUSTER

First published in Great Britain in 2018 by Simon and Schuster UK Ltd
A CBS COMPANY

Text Copyright © Passion Projects Limited 2018
Illustrations Copyright © Daniela Jaglenka Terrazzini

3 5 7 9 10 8 6 4 2

Simon & Schuster UK Ltd
1st Floor, 222 Gray's Inn Road
London
WC1X 8HB

www.simonandschuster.co.uk

Simon & Schuster Australia, Sydney
Simon & Schuster India, New Delhi

A CIP catalogue record for this book is available from the British Library.

PB ISBN 978-1-4711-7154-3
eBook ISBN 978-1-4711-7155-0
Audio 978-1-4711-7696-8

Printed and bound by CPI Group (UK) Ltd, Croydon, CR0 4YY

MIX
Paper from
responsible sources
FSC® C020471
www.fsc.org

For Jackson, Harrison and Lana

Chapter One

When I was small, one of my friends said something really silly. He said that Father Christmas didn't exist.

'So where do all the Christmas presents come from?' I asked him. He didn't have an answer.

'I don't know,' he said. 'It's just something my older sister told me.'

'Who comes down the chimney and eats the mince pies and drinks the brandy?' I asked. 'Who rides the sleigh?'

My friend was silent for a while.

'You know what?' he said. 'You're right. I don't know why I brought it up. Do you want to play marbles?'

That night, I had trouble getting to sleep. I had won the argument, but my friend had planted a tiny seed of doubt in my mind. What if Father Christmas *wasn't* real?

As Christmas approached, I began to ask myself all sorts of worrying questions: who *was* Father Christmas? Why did he bring presents? How did he deliver them all in one night? How did it all start?

I made up my mind that there was only one way to find out the truth. I had to meet Father Christmas, face to face.

Of course, I didn't tell anyone about my plan. My parents would have tried to stop me, and my twin sisters would have wanted to tag along, even though they were much too young. This was a serious operation and I couldn't risk it going wrong.

Finally, Christmas Eve arrived, and my parents came up to kiss me goodnight.

'Do you know what day it is tomorrow?' asked my mother, her eyes twinkling.

'Is it Wednesday?' I asked, pretending not to care.

She looked at my father, who shrugged.

'Yes, darling,' she said, trying to maintain an air of suspense. 'It is Wednesday. But it's also Christmas Day.'

'Oh,' I said. 'I'm not really that interested in Christmas.'

'Really?' said my father. They both looked very disappointed, and for a very brief moment I felt bad for tricking them.

'It's okay, I suppose,' I said, 'if you like presents and chocolate and sweets and things like that, but I prefer to work through a few maths problems while listening to classical music.' And then I faked a big yawn and closed my eyes.

'Whatever makes you happy, darling,' said my mother, sounding worried. They kissed me goodnight, switched out the light, and went downstairs.

I lay there in the dark, with my eyes closed, listening. I could hear my sisters in their bedroom down the hall, talking in their own special made-up language, which only they could understand. Usually, when I heard them talking like that it made me feel a bit left out, but not tonight, because I knew that I was doing something very special.

Eventually, my sisters fell quiet and the house suddenly seemed very deep and dark. I could hear the low murmur of my parents talking downstairs, but soon that stopped too, and then the stairs creaked as they made their way up to bed.

I knew they might look in on me, so I acted as if I was fast asleep.

'Goodnight, little man,' my father whispered, as he gently moved my head back on to the pillow and pulled the covers up to keep me warm. Then I smelled my mother's perfume as she gave me a kiss. The door closed, and I heard their footsteps crossing the landing to their bedroom.

I lay still, listening in the darkness. After what felt like the longest time, I decided it was safe enough to half-open one eye. My bedside clock showed a quarter to twelve. I had never, ever been awake that late before, and I wondered for a moment if, when it struck midnight, I would be turned to stone, like a child in a fairy tale.

I pulled back the covers, swung my feet

down on to the rug and tiptoed to the window. Outside, the window ledge was covered in snow. The moon was thin but bright, and in our neighbour's garden a fox picked its way across the white lawn. Above me, the blue-black sky was scattered with stars and little wisps of cloud. Nothing moved. No shooting stars, no satellites, not even a trundling planet. And definitely no reindeer-drawn sleigh.

I slunk back into bed. Using both pillows, together with one of the cushions from the chair, I made a sort of bed-throne, so that I could sit up and watch the open sky. Whatever happened, I wasn't going to sleep. I was going to wait until Father Christmas came.

It was the bells I heard first. I had expected

A fox picked its way across the white lawn.

jingle bells, like the ones in the song, but these sounded more like Alpine cowbells. I ran to the window. The sky was empty, just as before. Way off in the distance I heard the bells stop and start, growing a little louder each time. Little by little, they grew closer, and my excitement mounted. Then, finally, when they were at their loudest, there was a huge bang, followed by a loud grinding and sliding, and the whole ceiling shook. I'd always thought Father Christmas arrived quietly, but I couldn't have been more wrong. No wonder he has to wait until everyone is fast asleep!

Quick as a flash, I pulled on my dressing gown, slid my feet into my slippers, snatched up my toy rabbit and ran downstairs. Bold as you like, I burst through the sitting-room door and rushed to the fireplace. Lumps of soot fell into the cold grate. Father Christmas was coming!

Or, at least, he was trying to. The soot kept falling, and up in the chimney there were the muffled sounds of a struggle.

'Urggghhh,' I heard him say. 'You'd think one person would clean their chimney on Christmas Eve, but, oh, no.'

There was a shout, followed by a falling noise, followed by a someone-getting-stuck-in-a-chimney noise. There was the sound of wriggling and muttering, and then a tiny figure fell into the fireplace.

I had always imagined Father Christmas to be a giant, but the creature in front of me was minute. He had a bit of a tummy, though he wasn't what you'd call fat. He wore an old-fashioned red velvet jacket, embroidered with green, with matching red velvet trousers and dark-brown leather boots. He also had pointy ears and a turned-up nose, with short curly white hair stuffed under a red velvet cap. Suddenly it struck me. Father Christmas wasn't a person at all. He was an *elf*!

'Oh!' I shouted, in shock.

'Ah!' shouted Father Christmas, and jumped in fright, knocking over the fire irons, stumbling backwards and landing flat on his bottom in the fireplace.

'Ow!' he said. 'My ankle! I think I've twisted it.'

'I'm so sorry,' I said, feeling very guilty. 'It's my fault for scaring you. Let me help you up.'

I took him by the arm and helped him to his feet.

'Ouch!' he said. 'I can't put any weight on it, look.'

He tried to stand but was obviously in quite a lot of pain, so I lifted him by his armpits and sat him in my father's armchair.

'Hello,' he said, trying to compose himself as he took me in with his bright blue eyes. 'Umm . . . I'm a . . . chimney inspector. From the council. And I've been told to inspect this chimney. I've had a look, and it's fine, so I'm going now. Thank you so much for your help.'

'A chimney inspector?' I asked, pointing at a box of Lego that was poking out of his sack. 'Are you sure?' He quickly pushed the Lego back inside the sack and looked at me defiantly.

'That?' he said. 'That's my Lego. Lots of grown-ups do Lego. It's a thing.'

'You can't fool me,' I said. 'I know who you are.'

'You do?'

'Of course,' I said, trying to keep my cool. I was, after all, in the presence of a global superstar. 'Everyone does. You're Father Christmas. Every year children write a Christmas list, with all the presents we'd like, and send it to you at the North Pole. You have a workshop, where your elves make the presents—'

'Woah, woah, woah,' he said. 'They aren't *my* elves. They're my *employees* and they come to the workshop because they want to.'

'Aha!' I said, with a clap of my hands. 'So you are Father Christmas!'

'Ah,' said the elf, looking like he'd been caught out.

'Shall I tell you what else I know about you?' I asked.

'I've a feeling you might,' he replied.

'Well, on Christmas Eve you load all the presents on to your sleigh and your nine reindeer, Prancer and Dancer, Donner and Blitzen, Comet and Cupid, Dasher and Vixen, plus Rudolph, pull it through the sky.'

'Go on,' he said.

'At each house, you land your sleigh on the roof and then climb down the chimney to leave the presents by the Christmas tree. Exactly like you're doing now. So you must be Father Christmas.'

'It's possible,' he said. 'It's very possible. In fact . . .' He took a long pause, and looked me right in the eye. 'You're right.'

And then he smiled. It was like someone had turned on a sunlamp. His eyes twinkled with kindness, and I felt a wave of happiness lift me like a toy boat in a bathtub. All my doubts were gone. Father Christmas was real, and here he was, in my very own house.

'You must be Jackson,' he said. 'Why are you up so late, when everyone else is sleeping?'

'I was waiting for you,' I said. 'I want to ask you a really important question. Can I?'

'Shoot,' said Father Christmas.

'Who are you?' I asked.

'Who am I?' asked Father Christmas.

'How did all this start? How did you *become* Father Christmas?'

Father Christmas nodded slowly, as if my curiosity ever so slightly impressed him. 'Do you really want to know?' He smiled.

'More than anything,' I replied.

'Are you super-triple-sure?' asked Father Christmas. 'It might not be the story you are expecting.'

'No good story is,' I said.

'That's true,' said Father Christmas. 'That's very true.' He poked a finger into a pocket of his waistcoat, and pulled out a silver pocket watch. 'Well, I am slightly ahead of schedule. I suppose . . .' Once again, he looked me right in the eye. 'I suppose, as you've been *very* good, I could tell it to you quickly.'

'Yes, please,' I said.

Now, one thing you need to know about me is that I have an extraordinary memory. I can remember the dates and times of every single meal I have ever eaten – cheese sandwich, mustard instead of pickle, twelve-thirty p.m. three Wednesdays ago, being one such example – and my memory means that when someone tells me something, I can repeat every single word in exact order, for ever.

So, when I say that this is what Father Christmas told me, well . . . it's as good as him telling it to you himself . . .

Chapter Two

O nce, a very long time ago, there was a
town near the North Pole, which was
home to most of the world's elves. For
as long as anyone could remember, almost all
of them had worked in the town's shoe factory,
which the famous entrepreneurial elf Grimm
Grimmsson had built up from scratch.

Elves, as I'm sure you know, are
superb shoemakers, using only the very
softest leather, which they cut and stitch
completely by hand. They are also very

good at magic, so each shoe fitted whoever bought it perfectly.

For centuries, no human shoemaker could make a shoe even a tenth as well as elves, so Grimm Grimmsson had no competition. But then humans invented machines that could make shoes almost as quickly and almost as well as those the elves made. Of course, the shoes which human machines made didn't magically fit your foot, but no one cared because they were really, really cheap.

Over time, humans started to forget all about elf shoes, and only bought ones made by machines. Soon, Grimm Grimmsson found it was costing more to run the factory than he was making from selling the shoes and – in a notorious scandal – he left the town in the middle of the night with his shoemakers' pension fund.

All the elves that had worked in the shoe

factory suddenly found themselves out of work overnight. With no wages to feed their families, and nothing for them to do, they soon began to lose heart. Eventually there were two kinds of elf in the town: rich and poor. Which brings me to the main character in my story, Torvil Christmas.

Torvil was most definitely one of the town's rich elves. In fact, as owner of its only toyshop, he had done rather well for himself. But whereas most people who make money are happy to share it with their family and friends, Torvil kept his fortune all to himself.

To be fair, Torvil had no family, and he had no friends. Raised in an

orphanage, he'd never known his mother and father, and had never really been close with anyone his whole life. Our story begins when Torvil was five hundred and six, long past the age when most elves settle down and start a family. Torvil, however, was still very much alone.

(By the way, elves generally live ten times as long as humans. They are considered to be babies until the age of ten, toddlers until the age of thirty, children until they are one hundred and twenty, teenagers until they are two hundred, and grown-ups at the age of three hundred and three.)

Not that Torvil seemed to mind being alone. Money, he'd discovered, could easily take the place of people. And the great thing about money was that it never let you down. If you counted up your fortune after breakfast, you could be sure that it would still be there when you counted it after lunch, and again when you counted it after supper, and again when you counted it one last time before you went to bed. People might come and go, but money was for ever. All you had to do was make sure you didn't spend any of it.

Not spending money was one of Torvil's favourite hobbies. There were no two ways about it: Torvil was *mean*. If an elf came into his shop looking to buy his son or daughter a birthday present, and was too poor to afford any of the beautiful toys, Torvil never helped them out by dropping his prices, or by slipping a pack of Star Wars cards into the elf's satchel when he wasn't looking.

'Please, Mr Christmas, show some kindness,' the customer would say, to which Torvil always made the same reply: 'Kindness, my good sir, doesn't pay my bills.'

Now, you might think that having Christmas as his actual surname would have made Torvil a big fan of the festive season, but you'd be wrong. Torvil really didn't like Christmas at all; he hated it. Every Christmas he could remember had been miserable, spent on his own in his empty, cold house, with no friends or family to visit, and without so much as a single Christmas card, let alone a present. As a result, everything that normal people love about Christmas really got on Torvil's nerves: Christmas trees, Advent calendars, people being nice to one another on public transport; all of them put him in a very bad mood indeed.

The only thing that Torvil *did* like about Christmas was the money he made. In fact – and I'm ashamed to tell you this – when Christmas was coming, and every elf in town was scrimping and saving to buy toys, Torvil would put his prices up! His was the only toyshop in town so no one had any choice but to pay the extra cost. For many of the elf children, whose parents were poor, that meant fewer presents. For some, whose parents were very poor, I'm sorry to say it meant no presents at all.

And that's the way things might have stayed, but for a rather extraordinary turn of events. Events that changed Torvil's life for ever. Events that – as you shall shortly see – changed your life too.

Chapter Three

Midwinter is a very special time at the North Pole. If you ever go there — and I recommend you pay it a visit at least once in your life — you will soon discover why. From the beginning of December until the end of January, the sun never rises. It's always dark, apart from at midday, when something very magical happens. For just a few minutes, the sky turns the most beautiful shade of blue. The elves call it a 'blue moment' and it is one of the most wondrous sights a person can see.

As Christmas approaches, the blue moment gets shorter and shorter, until a week before the big day, when it stops happening altogether. Imagine that! For seven whole days and seven whole nights, everything is pitch black, all the time, and everyone begins to wonder whether they will ever see light again. Then, as if by magic, on Christmas Day, the blue moment returns.

A whole week of darkness might make a soul gloomy, if not downright depressed, so the elves have done something very clever. Instead of sitting at home, worrying about where the blue moment has gone, they celebrate. The dark days leading up to Christmas become increasingly jolly, and Christmas Eve is the most fun of all.

Everyone dresses up in their finest red velvet, drinks a special drink called mead, and generally has a high old time.

Needless to say, grumpy Torvil didn't care for such merry-making. He wore red velvet because he hated to stand out (and because he had bought a red velvet trouser suit as a young elf and was determined to get plenty of wear out of it), but that was all. He avoided the street parties, and he most definitely didn't drink mead. As far as he was concerned, the Christmas holiday was just another excuse for lazy elves to take time off work, and generally make a nuisance of themselves.

On one particular Christmas Eve, however, something rather remarkable happened. Excited by the prospect of selling a great number of toys, Torvil had woken early, and caught the first horse-sleigh into town. But as he snuck down the high street, doing his best to avoid the street-sellers and merry-makers, the sound of an old elfin sack-pipe caught his ear. He wasn't usually one for sack-pipes, or music at all for

27

that matter, but the melody he heard drifting through the sharp winter air seemed oddly familiar. And what was even odder was that it was coming from right outside his toyshop!

Sure enough, huddled outside the front window was a little group of elves, all singing at the tops of their voices.

'That's odd,' he whispered to himself. 'I think I know that tune.' Like an elf in a trance, he pushed his way to the centre of the circle. There, floating in mid-air, was the sack-pipe, seemingly playing all of its own accord. Beside it stood a Copper Elf with red hair and bright green eyes, holding a large brown felt hat, full of pennies.

Torvil's eyes narrowed. He was always suspicious of Copper Elves. They had some of the strongest elf magic, but never seemed to use it to good purpose. Magic, Torvil believed, should only ever be used responsibly. He wielded his to

There, floating in mid-air, was the sack-pipe, seemingly playing of its own accord.

run an efficient business and keep his bills low, not to amuse elves on the street.

With a flourish, the pipe sang one final note and collapsed in a heap on the floor. 'Penny for the carol singers?' called the Copper Elf through the letterbox.

'It's no good,' said a young elf, flapping his arms to try and keep warm. 'A very mean elf owns this shop, the meanest in the whole North Pole. He never gives us any money.'

Suddenly, Torvil came to his senses. The young elf was talking about him! Was this how people spoke of him behind his back? Without thinking twice, he pulled his scarf up around his face, in case any of them recognised him.

'Maybe he didn't like our singing,' said a voice in the crowd.

'I think we peaked at the butcher's,' sighed another.

Disheartened, the group of elves drifted off,

and the Copper Elf began to pack away the sack-pipe. Soon, only Torvil was left. Part of him wondered whether he should drift off too, and come back when the coast was clear. But another part of him wanted to know more about the tune.

'That's a shame,' he said to the Copper Elf. 'Seems like there's no one home.'

'What's that?' came the reply. 'Sorry, I can't hear what you're saying.'

'I said, it seems like there's no one home,' said Torvil, holding the scarf away from his mouth so that he could get the words out more clearly.

'Oh, they're home all right,' said the Copper Elf with a twinkle in his eye. 'At least, the pipe seems to think so.'

At that moment, the sack-pipe rose from its box like an octopus escaping from an aquarium, floated over towards Torvil, and began to play again.

'I really don't know why it's doing that,' said Torvil.

The Copper Elf frowned. 'This wouldn't be your shop, would it?' he asked.

'Oh!' said Torvil. 'No, no, no. I am far too poor an elf to own a grand shop like this. Though I have to say,' he said, stepping back and taking in the window display, 'they do have some spectacular offers on.'

Ignoring him, the Copper Elf simply held out the collection hat and shook it. 'Penny for the carol singers?' he said with a sinister grin, as the coins inside jingled.

'You're right, this is my shop,' said Torvil, lowering the scarf. 'I just felt a bit embarrassed because I don't have any money on me.'

'Nothing?' asked the Copper Elf.

'Nothing,' Torvil replied, rather unconvincingly.

'Then you'd better have this,' said the Copper

Elf, plucking a coin from his hat and tossing it in Torvil's direction. Torvil fumbled, and it landed in the snow.

'May it keep you as you deserve to be kept,' said the Copper Elf. By the time Torvil had found the coin, the Copper Elf was gone.

Chapter Four

Torvil's conversation with the Copper Elf had been rather unsettling and, despite the promise of a brisk day's trading, upon entering his shop, he found himself in a rather discontented mood. To make matters worse, his Toymaking Elf, Steinar, was nowhere to be seen.

Torvil frowned. Whenever he sold a toy, Steinar would magically make another one straight away to replace it so that the shelves were never empty. How could he be late on Christmas Eve, of all days? He should already be there making toys so that Torvil could make as much money as possible. Where on earth was he?

In fact, Steinar was at the butcher's shop in a rather large queue, hoping to buy a goose for his family's Christmas dinner. The money that Torvil paid him was barely enough to make ends meet, especially since his only daughter, Kiti, had become ill and often needed expensive medicine. But Steinar wanted to make his wife and daughter happy, so he was hoping the butcher would be willing to part with his smallest goose for just a few pennies.

Unfortunately, the butcher was not in a good mood either. Despite the big queue promising lots of profit for the shop that day, he had no patience for anything: not for his poor grown-up daughter, Gerda, who was serving with him, and certainly not for hard-up elves without money to spend.

'How much have you got?' he asked Steinar bluntly, so that all the other customers could hear.

'Two crowns,' said Steinar.

'Cheapest goose is twelve,' said the butcher. 'Next!'

Feeling like a failure, Steinar wandered back on to the snow-covered street wondering how he would tell his dear wife, Freya, that they would have nothing to eat for Christmas dinner. And what about poor Kiti, who was so excited about the festivities? Steinar tried hard to think positive thoughts, but it was no use, and a large hot tear rolled down his nose and drilled a tiny hole in a snowdrift.

Suddenly, he felt a gentle hand on his shoulder. It was Gerda. She had a kind, open face, and her long blonde hair was tied back with a pretty red-velvet ribbon.

'Here,' she said, putting a small package in his hand. 'Happy Christmas.'

Before Steinar could think to thank her, she kissed him on the forehead and went back inside the shop.

Stunned, Steinar undid the string on the package. There, nestling in the shiny brown paper, were half a dozen of the finest beef sausages he had ever seen. He couldn't believe his luck. What a Christmas dinner this was going to make! His family would be thrilled! He looked through the window at Gerda, who was

busy serving customers again.

'Thank you,' he said, clasping his hands to his chest, so that even though Gerda couldn't hear him she would know what he was saying. Gerda waved and smiled a big smile.

No sooner had Steinar gone than Gerda felt a hand on her own shoulder. She turned to find her father's red face right next to hers.

'What did you give him?' he asked threateningly.

'Just a couple of sausages,' said Gerda. 'He looked so sad and it is Christmas, after all.'

The butcher nodded slowly. 'Come with me,' he said taking her by the elbow and leading her to the office at the back of the shop. 'Here,' he said, pointing at an old ledger book on the desk. 'Here is everything it's cost me to raise you. Every meal, every pair of socks, every night you've stayed in my house. Look, see how much you owe me.'

Gerda looked up the number. 'Two hundred and ninety-three thousand, eight hundred and twenty-four crowns, Father,' she said meekly.

'Good girl,' said the butcher. 'Now, add the price of the sausages.' And Gerda did exactly as she was told.

Chapter Five

'What time do you call this?' asked Torvil, when Steinar arrived back from the butcher's shop.

'An inexcusably late one, master,' said Steinar. 'I'm so sorry, I got held up at the butcher's.'

'*Humph*,' said Torvil, scanning the street for customers. 'Squandering your wages on steak, no doubt. Learn to love the vegetable, Steinar! It's better for your health *and* your purse.'

Steinar wanted to say that his low wages meant that once he'd paid for Kiti's medicine, he could barely afford a carrot, but he thought better of it. Instead, he wiped the snow off his boots and followed Torvil into the wonderland that was the toyshop.

Seeing the toys he had made on display always gave Steinar a burst of bittersweet pride. There they were, the bright wooden building blocks, the toy sewing machines and rocking horses, the play castles and popguns. Steinar knew every screw and rivet, every varnish and paint job, every piece of ash and leather just as well as he knew the hairs on Kiti's head. It delighted him that they were so perfect, and saddened him that so few elf children could afford them.

'Now, before you start on those roller skates,' said Torvil sternly, 'I need your help. We have to up our prices, lickety-split, before all the Christmas shoppers arrive. Check the label of every toy, double the price, and magic a new label to replace the old one.'

'Yes, master,' said Steinar, unlocking the door to his workshop. Well, I say 'workshop'; really, it was more of a cupboard. Crammed inside were all the things Steinar needed to make his toys: lathes, vices, angle-poise lamps and soldering irons, as well as a bewildering variety of felts, paints, strings, glues, silver buttons and sequins made from mother-of-pearl.

Steinar placed the brown parcel of sausages on his desk, and looked at it thoughtfully. Now that he had something to cook for Christmas dinner, he needed to ask Torvil a question.

'Ahem,' he said, approaching the shop counter, where Torvil was counting out the day's cash float. 'I was wondering . . .'

'Yes?' said Torvil, without looking up.

'I know I asked this last year . . . and the year before that . . . in fact, I've asked every year . . .

you must be so bored of me! But I just wondered . . . Would it be at all possible for me to have the day off tomorrow?'

'Out of the question,' said Torvil, emptying a bag of coins on to the table.

'It's just . . . I'd like to spend Christmas with my family.'

'Forty-six, forty-seven . . .' said Torvil, counting under his breath.

'And there won't be any customers,' tried Steinar. 'Because it's a holiday. The shop will be empty.'

'Exactly,' said Torvil, glancing up at the toymaker. 'So it's the perfect day to take inventory, noting down every toy in the shop. Business is all about the bottom line, Steinar,' said Torvil, as he placed each coin in its correct compartment. 'To raise your profits, you need to lower your costs. Knowing every toy – what sells, what doesn't, which toys I can charge more for, which are a waste of time – that's why I'm so successful!' And, with that, he shut the till with a ringing sound that neatly emphasised his point.

'You forgot one,' said Steinar.

'What?' said Torvil, slightly annoyed that Steinar had ruined his big speech.

'You missed a penny,' said Steinar.

There, on the counter, was the silver coin given to him by the Copper Elf.

Torvil frowned. 'Hmm,' he said. At the end of the counter was a rickety mechanical arm with a magnifying glass on the end, which he often used for changing the insanely small screws that hold batteries in place on so many plastic toys. He pulled the magnifying glass towards him, and studied the coin closely.

It was old. Older than any coin he had

seen before and covered in strange early-elfin symbols. It must be valuable, surely? He chuckled to himself. What a fool that Copper Elf was! He probably had no idea how valuable it was and had given it away!

'What do you make of this?' he said to Steinar, showing off.

Steinar shook his head. 'Never seen anything like it.'

'Ha!' said Torvil, greatly pleased. 'Now face the other way.'

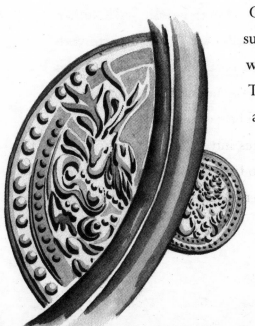

Once he was sure that Steinar wasn't looking, Torvil turned to a painting with an ornate gilt frame. It was hinged on one side, and Torvil swung it open to reveal a safe. Dialling in the correct combination, he carefully placed the coin inside, with the rest of his mountains of cash. Then, he locked the safe and pushed the picture frame back into place.

'Carry on,' said Torvil. And that was exactly what Steinar did.

It was one of the busiest Christmas Eves Torvil could remember. Skittle sets and leather footballs, toy swords and dolls' prams were flying off the shelves, and it was as much as Torvil could do to keep track of them all. At one point, the cash till became so full that he had to start stuffing notes into his Wellington boots, and Steinar had to fire up the kiln to bake more porcelain dolls to replace the ones that had been bought from the shop window.

Just as Torvil was ushering the last of the shoppers to the door, it started to snow. Cold-hearted though he was, even Torvil loved the sight of giant snowflakes settling on the fir trees and wooden roofs, and together with the thought of all the money he had made, he began to feel just a tiny bit generous.

'Do you know what?' he said to Steinar. 'I think I've been a little too miserly these past few months. Seeing all this snow has reminded me that it's Christmas. And Christmas is a time for generosity,' he said.

'Really, master?' said Steinar.

'A time to reward hard work and live a little.'

'Quite so, master,' said Steinar, allowing himself to hope.

'So, as it's snowing, I've decided to treat myself to a dog sled home. Be a good elf and hire one for me, would you? I'll bring it back first thing in the morning.'

Steinar's smile froze as he tried not to let his disappointment show. He had thought that, perhaps, just once, Torvil might show some kindness and Christmas spirit and allow him the day off, or even just a little extra money for all his hard labour. But really he should have known better.

'Yes, of course, master,' he said. 'It would be my pleasure.' And out he went into the blizzard.

With Steinar gone, Torvil had just the chance he needed to stash away all the day's takings. The safe was full, almost to overflowing, and he kept having to push the money back inside so that he could close the door.

'Ready and waiting, master,' said Steinar, shaking the snow from his hat as he entered the shop.

'Excellent,' said Torvil.

Steinar unfolded an umbrella and held it over Torvil's head as Torvil locked the door of the shop and clambered on to the back of the empty dog sled.

'Are you sure you don't want a driver, master?' Steinar asked. 'It's bitter cold out there.'

'And pay nearly twice the price?' said Torvil with a sneer. 'I am quite capable of steering my own sled, thank you very much. See you tomorrow at eight o'clock sharp!' he said to Steinar, and with a '*Yah!*' he cracked the reins, and disappeared into the snowstorm.

Chapter Six

I f you ever do go to the North Pole – and on that subject I feel I have made my feelings clear – then you absolutely have to ride on a sled pulled by huskies.

There's nothing like tearing through the muffled silence of a snowy town at night, with fat snowflakes sinking like galleons and the icy wind nipping at your cheeks. A husky is never happier than when it is running as part of a pack, and it's almost impossible not to feel the excitement of the dogs as they take off across

51

the snow.

Torvil was far too miserable at heart to really feel alive, but that evening as he sledded home, he came pretty close. There were still revellers in the high street, and the dogs wove expertly among them as they pounded first past the post office, then the bakery, then the butcher's shop. As he raced past, Torvil glimpsed Gerda in the bright window, scrubbing the chopping block in the sink while the butcher barked orders from the counter. Torvil had known Gerda in his youth, and for a moment he felt a pang of sadness that they were no longer friends. He felt the urge to wave to her, and had half-raised one arm when one of the huskies lost its footing, the sled jolted, and he was needed at the reins.

After the high street, the road began to climb, and Torvil had to crack the whip to keep the dogs working. This was where the rich elves lived, and he passed the lights of large wooden cabins, where young elves in brushed cotton pyjamas were saying goodnight to their well-groomed parents, and sprightly older elves were reading to one another by the fire. Then, one by one, the houses began to fall away, and Torvil passed the darkness of the town's derelict orphanage. Up here on the hill the air was clear and still, and for a few brief seconds a hazy full moon lit the path. Next came a few solitary fir trees, then a gaggle, and then the road plunged into dense forest.

'*Yah*!' Torvil called to the dogs once more, and they began to pick up speed. The trees pressed closer, and the track began to weave wildly from left to right, as they raced deeper and deeper into the forest. Torvil was beginning to wonder whether he might be going a tiny bit too fast when he rounded a corner to find the path ahead completely blocked by an enormous reindeer.

There's a strange thing that happens when you have an accident at high speed (as I hope you never find out): time expands and split-seconds drag out into what feels like minutes. In what seemed like the slowest of slow motion, Torvil threw himself to the ground and proceeded to slide head-first right between the reindeer's legs and out the other side. The last thing he could remember was a large tree trunk ploughing towards him like the periscope of a submerged submarine, followed by black.

Chapter Seven

'Ah,' said Father Christmas. He glanced at his watch, and then at his sack of presents. 'Erm . . . I think we might have to pick this up another time.'

'What?' I asked, horrified at the interruption. 'But . . . what happens next?'

'A lot of things,' said Father Christmas. 'That's why it's such a good story.'

'But . . . but . . .' I said, searching for any reason to make him stay. 'You said you were ahead of schedule.'

'I was, and now I'm not,' said Father Christmas, rising from the footstool where he had been sitting. 'And this tale is much too good to rush. OW!'

'Is everything all right?' I asked, suspecting that it probably wasn't.

'My ankle!' he said, hopping around on one leg. 'AH!'

I remembered when my father had twisted his ankle during the parents' egg-and-spoon race at my last sports day. 'Take off your boot!' I said and raced to the kitchen, grabbed a bag of frozen peas, and raced back again.

Father Christmas gave a sharp intake of breath as I wrapped the peas around what I have to tell you was a rather sweaty sock. 'Ow!' he said. 'That's freezing!'

'Sorry,' I said, feeling like this was all my fault. 'But I promise this will make the swelling go down.'

'This is bad,' said Father Christmas. 'This is very bad. How am I going to deliver my presents?'

'Can I help?' I asked.

'How?' asked Father Christmas.

'I could carry you?'

There was a pause while Father Christmas considered what I can only describe as a limited range of options.

'Let's try it,' he said, shouldering his sack of presents. I lifted him on to the chair, and he clambered on to my back. I did my best to stand, but the sack was much too heavy, and I had to plonk him down again before I toppled over backwards.

'It's no good,' he said. 'This is never going to work.'

'Wait,' I said. 'What if you sit on my shoulders,

and balance the sack on my head?'

There was another pause.

'That,' said Father Christmas, nodding slowly, 'might be a very good idea indeed.'

Seconds later, we were on the roof. There, standing in the moonlight, was the largest sleigh I had ever seen in my life. It was the size of a lorry and half-buried under a landslide of presents. Harnessed in front of it were nine enormous reindeer, pawing the ground, breathing out huge clouds of steamy breath, and shaking their antlers, so that the large bells around their necks rang out in the night. Father Christmas led me straight to the leader of the pack, an enormous grey-brown beast with a very runny pinkish nose. I knew at once that this must be Rudolph.

'Here he is,' said Father Christmas, feeding Rudolph the carrot. 'My secret weapon.'

'Because of his shiny nose?' I asked breathlessly, partly in wonder, and partly because I had just carried Father Christmas up four flights of stairs.

'Not really,' said Father Christmas, passing the carrot around to the other reindeer so they could all have a nibble. 'In fact, that's a major drawback. He's always got a cold and passes his germs on to the other reindeer. No, he's my secret weapon because he can fly.'

'He can hear as well,' said Rudolph matter-of-factly.

'Sorry, Rudolph,' said Father Christmas.

'Apology accepted,' said Rudolph. 'Although for your information, it's not a cold, it's flu. I've got the shivers and my joints ache. Who's this?'

'This is Jackson. He's going to help me on my

rounds tonight.'

'Is that a good idea?' said Rudolph. 'No one ever comes with us.'

'He has to,' said Father Christmas. 'I've twisted my ankle and without him, I can't deliver the presents.'

'And Father Christmas is telling me a story,' I said proudly. 'It's about Torvil the elf.'

'Ah, then he must have told you how we met?' said Rudolph.

'*Ssshh, sshhh, sshhh!*' said Father Christmas. 'You'll spoil it. Anyway, as I was saying, Rudolph is my secret weapon because he can fly. Without him, we'd never get off the ground. Now, let's get going; we've got a lot of places still to visit.'

I helped Father Christmas on to the seat of the sleigh, then clambered up beside him. I pulled a bearskin rug over our knees, and Father Christmas took up the reins.

'*Yah!*' he cried. '*Yah!*'

'Come on, guys!' called Rudolph to the other reindeer, swallowing hard. 'Let's do this!'

As one, the nine reindeer leaned into their harnesses, and dragged us in a wide circle until we were facing the edge of the roof.

'Hang on tight!' whispered Father Christmas.

'Here we go!' called Rudolph. 'Three, two, one . . . charge!'

The reindeer strained as they took the full weight of the sleigh. For a brief moment, it felt as if it might be too much for them. Then, all of a sudden, we lurched forward and began to rapidly accelerate. If you have ever been in a plane when it takes off, it was a little bit like that, except we weren't wearing seatbelts and no one had shown us the emergency exits.

I was expecting us to lift off high into the night sky, but the instant we cleared the edge we toppled downward, dropping like a stone, and it was only when I thought we were bound to crash that the sleigh began to heave and creak and we surged back up again. We rammed into the top of a large tree, scattering snow and pine needles, and soon the lights of the city were spread out before us.

We were flying!

'Sorry about that,' said Father Christmas. 'My fault. If they have too long a break they start to lose the knack.'

'Where are we going?' I asked.

'Africa,' said Father Christmas. 'Do you know which direction that is?'

'South?' I asked.

'Exactly,' said Father Christmas. 'Eight thousand and thirty-one kilometres away, to be precise. We should be there in eight minutes and seventeen seconds. Look! The Houses of

Parliament!'

I looked to where he was pointing, and instantly regretted it, because a split-second later we flew so close to the clock on Big Ben that I nearly jumped out of my seat.

'*Yah!*' called Father Christmas. '*Yah!*'

'Yes, we get it!' shouted Rudolph.

We plunged into a bank of cloud, and I looked at Father Christmas in concern.

'Don't worry,' called Father Christmas. 'Rudolph knows where he's going.'

A few minutes later, the stars reappeared, and London became a fizzing web of yellow light far behind us.

'Now, we have a bit of time until we land, so where were we in our story?' he called.

'Torvil the elf,' I said, battling against a gust of wind, 'he's just hit a tree and been knocked out.'

'Impressive,' said Father Christmas. 'You really listened. Well, this is what happened next.'

And this, pretty much word for word, is what he told me . . .

Chapter Eight

When he finally opened his eyes, Torvil found that he was lying flat on his back in the snow, staring up at a clear, moonless sky, littered with stars. What's more, he had a very bad headache.

He felt something cold on his face. Was he bleeding? Tenderly he pulled the glove from his left hand, stroked his cheek, and squinted at the tips of his fingers to see if they were red. They weren't, but they were covered in slobber.

It was at that point the reindeer decided to

lick him again.

'Eww!' said Torvil, wiping his face with the back of his sleeve. 'Shoo!' he said, waving his arms.

The reindeer looked at him in surprise. 'I'm sorry,' it said. 'I'm guessing you're not very tactile? Though you are alive, which is a bonus.'

Torvil, who had never met a talking reindeer before, stared back in disbelief.

'What's the problem?' said the reindeer. 'Have I got a bit of lichen in my teeth? Where's a frozen puddle when you need one, eh? Ah! Here we go . . .'

Taking a deep breath, he blew the snow off a small section of ice very close to Torvil's face, and examined his front teeth. 'Negatory, officer,' he said in an official voice, 'that is one clean grill.' And then, 'Sorry, I seem to have caught you with a couple of snowflakes there,' he said, huffing the snow from where it had settled on Torvil's glasses.

Torvil continued to stare, not quite sure

'That is one clean grill.'

what to say.

'Oh,' said the reindeer. 'It's the talking thing, isn't it? I always forget. People say to me, "It's amazing that you can talk!" and I say, "Anyone can talk. What's amazing is that I can *connect*."'

Wondering if his bump on the head had somehow affected his brain, Torvil decided to try and stand up. He stretched his toes and fingers to check everything was working properly, then took a deep breath and hauled himself to his feet using the lower branches of a nearby sapling. It was then that he noticed something very odd. The snow around him was freshly fallen, with no sign of the crash.

'Hang on,' he said, trying to make sense of it all. 'Where's the sled?'

'It doesn't exist yet,' said the reindeer with a shrug.

'Excuse me?' said Torvil, thinking he must

have misheard.

'Well, not as a sled,' said the reindeer. 'The wood exists. In fact, that's it right there.' And with its rather sore-looking nose, the reindeer pointed to the sapling fir tree that Torvil was now propped up against.

'What in the great wide Pole are you talking about?' asked Torvil. How could the sled he had just crashed not yet exist?

'This tree becomes the dog sled,' explained the reindeer, speaking slowly, as if Torvil was a small child. 'It grows big and tall, then gets cut down by a Woodcutter Elf, then turned into planks by a Lumber Elf, and then carved by a Woodworking Elf.'

'Turned into planks?' asked Torvil, more confused than ever. 'There's not enough wood here to make a box of matches.'

'Not now there isn't,' agreed the reindeer.

'But in five hundred years' time there will be.'

'Say that again?' asked Torvil.

'We're five hundred years in the past,' said the reindeer, wiping a sniffle from its red nose with one of its knees. 'Five hundred and six, to be precise.'

'Stuff and nonsense,' said Torvil. 'I must have hit my head harder than I thought! Well, I can't walk home from here, it'll take all night. I'll go back into town and hire another dog sled. I'll probably be charged a fortune for losing this one!'

And, with that, Torvil gave a big humph and strode back towards the town.

Chapter Nine

At least, that's what he tried to do. What actually happened was that Torvil took one step forward and sank right up to his neck in a snowdrift.

'Ah, yes. It is quite deep there,' said the reindeer. 'Do you need a bit of help?'

'Absolutely not,' said Torvil. 'I knew the snow was deep. If it's any business of yours, which I strongly suspect it isn't, I felt a little hot and bothered after my accident and I thought this would be an efficient way to cool down.

In a moment, when my body temperature has reached a comfortable level, I shall be on my . . . Wait a minute . . .'

With some difficulty, Torvil looked up at the reindeer, who was now standing right beside him.

'Why aren't *you* sinking?' asked Torvil.

'I float,' said the reindeer.

'You do *what?*' said Torvil.

'I'm a . . . you know . . . flying reindeer. You see these shoes?' he said, picking up one of his hooves.

'That's close enough, thank you,' said Torvil, who didn't much like having a large reindeer hoof shoved in his face.

'Any idea what these are made of?' asked the reindeer.

'Please do tell me,' said Torvil.

'Osmium,' said the reindeer. 'Twice as dense

as lead. That one there,' he said, waving his hoof right under Torvil's nose, 'weighs the same as a bucket of sand. Without them I'd shoot up into the sky like a hot air balloon. With them on, I'm balanced just right.'

'Really?' said Torvil. 'Are you sure you aren't just standing on a snow-covered rock?'

'Suit yourself,' said the reindeer and, reaching down, he gripped the fur collar of Torvil's jacket between his teeth, and began to pull Torvil up on to the surface of the snow.

'Ow!' said Torvil. 'You've got my neck hair!'

'Just relax,' said the reindeer. 'We'll have you out of there in no time.'

'Stop it!' shouted Torvil. 'Stop it! Let go of me this instant!'

'Honestly,' said the reindeer, dropping him like a stone. 'I was only trying to help!'

'I don't need any more of your "help",

73

thank you very much,' said Torvil, struggling to his feet. 'Goodbye!'

Chapter Ten

The snow on the track was deep, and Torvil found the walk back up the hill extremely tiring. Luckily, the stars were bright and there was very little cloud, which meant there was just enough light to see by. If he hadn't been in such a bad mood, Torvil might have marvelled at how still and silent the forest was, how his breath hung in the air like smoke, and how the tiny ice crystals on the snow-covered branches sparkled like fairy dust.

Soon he saw the glow of the town lighting

the clouds ahead of him and, as he grew closer, he heard the distant beating of elfin drums. Clearly the Christmas revels were still in full swing. No doubt the streets were packed with rosy-cheeked elves, dancing and making merry, careless of the worries of the world.

The thought made Torvil shudder. He would have to pass through the crowds on his way to the sled-hire shop. What if someone tried to dance with him, or make him sing? He stopped in his tracks. As deep as the snow was, maybe it was worth walking all the way home, after all . . .

He was about to turn around when he noticed something very odd on the road beside him. Just visible through the trees was the outline of the abandoned orphanage. For as long as he could remember, it had been empty, cold and unloved, surrounded by a tall, locked, rusting iron fence.

But now there was something very different about it. All the lights were on.

He frowned and waded more quickly through the snow, curious to see what might be going on. Had a band of drunk elves decided to take it over for a party? If so, he would lodge an official complaint with the town elders. The building was old and dangerous, with slates missing from the roof and rubble in its grounds, and he was sure that a party would be against health and safety regulations. This, he told himself, was the whole problem with allowing elves to enjoy themselves. They were never content with a nibble of acorn cake and a sip of silver bark tea. They always had to take it too far.

But Torvil was wrong. As he drew closer, it was clear that the orphanage, far from being derelict, was the picture of health. There were painted shutters on the windows, and the snow had been cleared from the path in a garden laid to lawn and late-flowering shrubbery. Through the windows he could see smartly dressed staff ushering boys and girls in dark-blue uniforms. The sight moved him greatly, and he almost smiled. Almost, because it was at that point he heard a baby crying.

At the gate, barely metres ahead of him, sat a wicker shopping basket. Edging closer, Torvil saw that the crying was coming from a rather cross-looking baby wrapped tightly in a hand-knitted blanket.

The reindeer nudged him. 'Mind-blowing, isn't it?' he said.

'Excuse me?' asked Torvil, who hadn't realised he was being followed.

'You know who that is, don't you?' said the reindeer.

Torvil peered at a label attached to the handle

of the basket. In clear handwriting was a single word: *Torvil.*

'It can't be,' said Torvil in a quiet voice. 'It's that bang on the head, it's sent me funny for sure. I passed by here ten minutes ago, and the whole place was deserted. No lights, no people, and definitely no baby.'

'I told you,' said the reindeer. 'We're in the *past.* And that's you. Left here at the orphanage gates.'

'That's not possible,' said Torvil. 'That's simply not possible.'

The baby, which had paused for breath, started crying again.

'I'm taking this poor child inside,' said Torvil, stepping forward to pick up the basket. But, just as his hand was about to close on the handle, the reindeer's teeth clamped down on his collar once again, and dragged him backwards through the snow.

'Would you please stop doing that?' exclaimed Torvil.

'It's against the rules,' said the reindeer.

'What rules?' asked Torvil.

'This is your past. You're not allowed to change it. All you can do is watch.'

As if to emphasise the reindeer's point, a gust of wind skittered past them, kicking up clouds of powdery snow. A handful of snowflakes found their way into the basket, and the baby began to cry even more loudly.

'Oh, this is absurd!' said Torvil, his heart melting a little. 'That poor baby!'

Thankfully, at that very moment, the door of the orphanage opened, and a young woman in uniform placed a crate of old-fashioned glass milk bottles on the doorstep.

'Over here!' called Torvil. 'Over here!'

'Ssssh!' said the reindeer, making an executive decision to butt Torvil backwards through a bush.

'Ow!' said Torvil.

'Keep down!' hissed the reindeer.

Over on the doorstep, the young woman turned and looked in their direction. Taking a lantern, she began to walk down the path towards them. She held the lantern high and scanned the ground beyond the gate, but could see nothing but a single bush, curiously free of snow. And then, finally, she saw the baby.

'I remember her,' whispered Torvil to the reindeer. 'That's Miss Turi. We liked her. She was very kind.'

As quickly as she could, Miss Turi opened the gate, lifted the baby from the basket, and held it close. She looked all around, but could see no sign of anyone that might have left it there. For the briefest of moments she looked straight at the bush where Torvil and the reindeer were hiding, and they had to crouch down even further to be sure they were out of sight. Then, seeing no one, Miss Turi closed the gate and hurried back to the orphanage, shutting the door behind her. Through the large staircase windows, Torvil saw her climbing, floor by floor, all the way to the eaves.

'Can you really fly?' Torvil asked.

'Only one way to find out,' said the reindeer as it aligned itself with a convenient tree stump. 'Come on. Up you hop.'

Before he had even paused to think how dangerous it might be to ride a flying reindeer with no saddle, no training, and no head for heights, Torvil set one foot on the tree stump and vaulted on to the reindeer's back. At which point, the reindeer turned and cantered towards the forest.

'What are you doing?' shouted Torvil, pointing at the orphanage. 'It's that way!'

'Everyone's an expert, aren't they?' said the reindeer, slowing to a halt. 'I need a run-up.'

And then he turned once more, and began to gallop at full speed towards the gates.

'Hold on tight!' the reindeer called, and just when it seemed he was going to smash headlong into the ironwork, he sprang from the ground like an event horse leaping a four-star fence. Up, up into the cold night they soared, with the reindeer's hooves pounding the air and Torvil hanging on for dear life!

Chapter Eleven

They landed with a clatter on the orphanage roof. Unfortunately, beneath their appealing covering of snow, the slates were rather slippery and, after trotting to what should have been an elegant halt, the reindeer continued to slide up and up the sloping roof, slowing under gravity until it crested the ridge, at which point it tipped ever-so-slowly forward and began to slide down the other side.

'What are you doing?' called Torvil.

'Panicking,' replied the reindeer. 'Bail!'

Torvil needed no further encouragement, and jumping from the reindeer's back, landed hard on his bottom. He and the reindeer were now sliding side by side, picking up speed, heading down towards the roof's edge.

'Quick!' called the reindeer. 'Grab the gutter!'

Torvil did as he was told, and the two of them executed a neat gymnastic move, flipping over the edge of the roof and landing with control on a window ledge beneath them.

Torvil and the reindeer looked at one another.

'Cool,' said the reindeer.

'*Sssh*!' whispered Torvil. 'Look.'

Inside was a long, narrow room, its ceiling criss-crossed with wooden beams, with beds full of sleeping children. Next to an empty cot there was a lit candle and a small pool of light.

Beside it, Miss Turi comforted the abandoned baby, while a stern-looking older woman fitted the cot with sheets and blankets.

'I remember her too,' whispered Torvil. 'That's Mrs Somby. We didn't like her quite so much.'

The two women were talking to one another, but it was impossible to make out what they were saying.

'Follow me,' hissed the reindeer, and he and Torvil shuffled along the ledge towards the next window, which happened to be open.

'What shall we call him?' Miss Turi was saying.

'Torvil, of course,' replied Mrs Somby, pointing to the label on the basket. 'Can't you read?'

'Torvil,' Miss Turi said, chalking the name on a small blackboard at the end of the cot. 'But what about his surname?'

'Hmm,' said Mrs Somby. 'Perhaps something plain like Korhonen or Nieminen?'

'We can't just give him any old surname,' said Miss Turi. 'It has to be something special to him.'

'Whatever,' said Mrs Somby, and headed for the door.

As if he could hear Mrs Somby's uncaring tone, baby Torvil started to cry.

'Sssh, Torvil, sssh,' said Miss Turi, stroking the baby's cheek. 'You'll have lots of friends here. Look, this is Gerda, she's going to be sleeping right next to you.' As she spoke, Miss Turi carried the baby over to a nearby cot with a name-board that read: *Gerda, 10 December.* Right on cue, baby Gerda opened her large brown eyes and smiled. And, as if greeting a new friend, baby Torvil stopped crying and smiled back.

It was then the reindeer noticed that grown-up Torvil had a tear in his eye. 'What is it?' whispered the reindeer.

'Gerda,' said Torvil, a tenderness in his voice. 'She was my friend.'

Miss Turi was humming the baby a lullaby. Of course! Now Torvil knew where he had heard the melody played by the Copper Elf's sack-pipe. It was the lullaby Miss Turi had sung to them at the orphanage.

Smiling, Miss Turi took up a piece of chalk, and wrote: *Christmas Eve* on the small blackboard at the end of baby Torvil's cot. As her chalk formed the final letter, a thought struck her.

'That's what your surname should be!' she said. 'Christmas. Torvil Christmas.'

She tucked baby Torvil safely under the covers, and blew out the candle.

On the window ledge, the wind picked up,

Miss Turi was humming the baby a lullaby.

blowing thick with snowflakes, and Torvil found he could hardly see his hand in front of his face.

'Hello?' he called, looking around for the reindeer.

'Torvil?' called the reindeer. 'Torvil!'

But it was too late. Suddenly, as if a rug had been pulled out from beneath their feet, the ledge disappeared from under them, and with a shout of alarm, Torvil and the reindeer began to fall.

Chapter Twelve

Down and down they fell, flailing and kicking, the white wind whistling all around them. Torvil had never fallen from the top floor of an orphanage before, so he had very little with which to compare the experience, but it seemed to him that they fell for a lot longer than was justified by everyday physics. He was half-beginning to wonder whether they might ever hit the ground at all when they landed flat on their backs in an enormous snowdrift.

It was what you might call a soft landing, but Torvil's relief was short-lived. He might have survived the fall, but he had sunk so deep that he was crushed by the sheer weight of snow on top of him. Summoning all his energy, he tried to sit up. It was useless. He tried to lift one leg, but he couldn't do that either. Last of all, he tried to lift his little finger, but even that was pinned down as if by a ten-tonne weight. At that point, he started to lose all hope.

'Reindeer, are you there?' he whispered.

'I have got a name, you know,' said the reindeer.

'I can't breathe,' said Torvil bravely. 'If I don't make it——'

'It's Rudolph,' interrupted the reindeer. 'My parents were German.'

'Right,' said Torvil, not really listening. 'If I don't make it, tell Gerda——' Torvil paused, his lips turning blue with lack of oxygen.

'Yes?' said Rudolph.

But Torvil, whose breath was almost spent, found it difficult to get any words out. All that came from his mouth was a wheezing sound, as if someone was expelling the last thimbleful of air from a flat sack-pipe.

'Tell Gerda what?' pushed the reindeer.

Now Torvil could no longer even wheeze. His life, he thought hopelessly, was probably numbered in seconds.

'Tell you what, I'll get off you, and see if that's any better,' Rudolph said and stood up. It was then that Torvil realised the reason he couldn't breathe was not because he was being crushed by a very great weight of snow, but because he was being sat on by a very great weight of reindeer.

'What are you doing, you great oaf?' Torvil

shouted. 'I could have suffocated under there!'

'It wasn't that comfortable for me, either,' said the reindeer, glancing through a ground-floor window as he spoke. 'You're a sack of bones. Seriously, you need to chub up a bi– Oh my days! Christmas, you need to see this.'

Cross as he was, Torvil joined the reindeer at the window.

At first, he couldn't see what the fuss was about. A dozen or so children sat, waiting patiently with empty bowls, while Mrs Somby served them supper. It was Gerda he recognised first, and as she held her bowl up for a ladle-full of grey liver, a shiver ran down his spine. She was beautiful and her eyes shone with kindness.

'Wait . . .' he said to the reindeer, 'We've jumped in time. And if that's Gerda . . . then–'

'The boy next to her is you,' said the reindeer, finishing his sentence. And sure enough, there he was. Though whereas the younger Gerda was easily recognisable, Torvil's younger self was alarmingly different. There was no hunch in his shoulders, no frown on his forehead: his posture was elegant, his eyes shone, and his tousled blond hair reached almost to his collar.

'Wait. I remember this,' said Torvil, recalling a distant memory. 'It was Christmas dinner. Usually we had a slice of bacon, but this one year it was liver. I couldn't eat it.'

Just as he spoke, the young Torvil made a face at Gerda and pushed his bowl to one side. Making sure no one was watching, Gerda took her bread from beside her plate and handed it to the young Torvil behind her back.

Across the table, Mrs Somby stopped ladling; she had seen Gerda's crime. 'Gerda! What was that you just passed to Torvil?'

Thankfully, at that very moment the door

burst open, and in came Miss Turi. She was carrying a hemp sack and – much to the dismay of Mrs Somby – all the children immediately threw down their spoons and ran to greet her. Smiling warmly, Miss Turi reached into the sack and handed each and every one of the children a small present wrapped in brown paper and tied with string. 'Don't get excited,' she said. 'They are just small things.'

'I'd forgotten this,' said Torvil to the reindeer, with a fondness in his voice. 'Miss Turi always used to make us presents.'

It was only a matter of seconds before all the children had unwrapped their little parcels. Inside hers, Gerda found a rag mouse. She gave a shriek of joy and clutched it tight. The young Torvil had a rag hedgehog. Other children unwrapped rag snakes, rag kittens and rag puppies, all of them made by

Miss Turi.

'Thank you, Miss Turi! You're the best!' they cried, and threw their arms around her.

'When I grow up,' said young Torvil eagerly, 'I'm going to be rich. Every Christmas I'm going to come back here and give all the children a present!'

'That sounds wonderful,' said Miss Turi, ruffling his hair. 'Happy Christmas, all of you! Now, I must go and give these last few gifts to the babies.'

As soon as she left the room, something terrible happened. Mrs Somby, who was not only cross with Gerda, but also furious that Miss Turi was so much more popular than she was, snatched Gerda's rag mouse, and threw it on the fire. Gerda was so shocked, she couldn't even cry.

'That's what happens to little girls who break the rules,' said Mrs Somby. 'No sharing!'

'That's so unfair!' muttered the reindeer.

'Welcome to the world,' replied Torvil.

'Wait a minute,' said the reindeer. 'Hero incoming . . .'

Turning back to the window, Torvil saw a little scene unfolding that filled him with pride.

'Cheer up,' said his younger self, putting a protective arm around the distraught Gerda. 'You can have my hedgehog. I don't want it.'

Gently, Gerda took the toy and held it close. 'Thank you,' she whispered. 'Promise you'll be my friend for ever?'

'Promise,' said young Torvil.

'Hmm,' said the reindeer, puzzled.

'Hmm, what?' asked Torvil.

'I don't get it. You were a good kid. Now you're just . . . awful. What's your deal?'

Torvil was about to answer, when he was almost blown clean over by another ice-cold blast of wind. No sooner had he recovered his balance than once again the air was bright with swirling snowflakes, as if the entire world was a snow-globe shaken by an angry giant. Then, as quickly as it had risen, the wind subsided, the snow settled, and a warm summer sun shone on the windows of the orphanage.

To stand in daylight again after weeks of darkness was magical, and for a moment Torvil could hardly take it all in. The trees in the orphanage garden bristled with icicles, and the frozen pond shone like a mirror. It appeared that once again, they had jumped forward in time. And, sure enough, when he and the reindeer approached the window, a new scene was unfolding beyond the glass.

All the chairs and tables had been cleared, and the orphans were sitting cross-legged on the floor, while Mrs Somby addressed them. Among them, Torvil could see his younger self and Gerda, now teenagers.

'These four couples each have room for one child,' Mrs Somby was saying.

The orphans began to chatter excitedly. Having their very own family would be a dream come true.

'Children, please!' Mrs Somby said with a forced smile, struggling to disguise her bad temper. 'Be patient. All will be revealed.'

'You want to know what my "deal" is?' said Torvil to the reindeer, in a low voice. 'Then watch this. This is when it all begins, when I start to learn what life is really like.'

The first of four couples took centre-stage. 'Mr and Mrs Nyqvuist,' said Mrs Somby self-importantly. 'Have you made your decision?'

'We have,' said Mr Nyqvuist. 'And we choose . . . Wilder.'

All the orphans at the back of the room burst into applause, and a red-headed boy stood up.

'Ah,' said the reindeer. 'That's so sad. They didn't choose you.'

'Sssh,' said Torvil. 'This is just the beginning.'

'Next,' Mrs Somby said, 'we have Mr and Mrs Bergmann.'

Mr and Mrs Bergmann looked at one another, then at Mr and Mrs Nyqvuist.

'Sorry, this is rather awkward . . .' said Mrs Bergmann, her voice trailing off in embarrassment. 'We wanted Wilder as well . . .'

'Would any of the other children do?' asked Mrs Somby.

Mr and Mrs Bergmann looked at one another again. 'I think we'll wait till the spring,' said Mr Bergmann. 'Just in case anything – I mean, any*one* – better comes in. I don't mean better, I mean . . . suitable. Anyone more suitable.'

'Understood,' said Mrs Somby.

'Ouch,' said the reindeer. 'That's got to hurt.'

Torvil was concentrating so hard on the scene that he didn't reply.

'Got it,' said the reindeer. 'There's more.'

Inside, Mrs Somby was presenting the third couple, a Mr and Mrs Ekelund.

'After much thought . . .' said Mr Ekelund, with a dramatic pause.

'We'd very much like to adopt . . .' continued Mrs Ekelund, taking an even longer pause.

'Ingrid!' exclaimed Mr Ekelund.

Once again, there was a burst of applause from the orphans, and a very pretty girl with her hair in plaits stood up.

'Though we would also like to give a favourable mention to Ranveig,' said Mr Ekelund, 'who we thought made excellent conversation during the meet-and-greet, and showed a lot of enthusiasm for housework during the tasks, but in the end just didn't quite have it in the looks stakes. Maybe lose the braces?' he said, pointing at his front teeth.

A little girl with curly brown hair burst into tears and buried her face in her hands.

'Here we go,' said Torvil, nudging the reindeer. 'This is it coming up now.'

'And Mrs Loven?' Mrs Somby was asking. 'I suppose you can't really make a decision as your husband isn't here.'

'On the contrary,' said Mrs Loven, her golden hair catching the light, 'I have never felt so sure of anything in all my life. You children are all so wonderful, and I wish I could take you all, but sadly, we only have room for one. And there is a child here with whom I felt a special bond. A generous, open-hearted boy who will make the perfect son. I choose . . . Torvil.'

Applause broke out in the middle of the room, and teenage Torvil, who hadn't dared to hope that he might be chosen, sat open-mouthed in shock. Gerda, who was sitting next to him, gave him a huge hug. 'Promise you'll come and visit?' she whispered, as he struggled to his feet.

'Mrs Loven,' he said, in a faltering voice. 'I'm so grateful. But as happy as I'll be to have a proper family, I'll miss my friend Gerda. Is there any way you could take us both?'

'The ingratitude!' roared Mrs Somby.

'The cheek!'

'Please, Mrs Somby,' said Mrs Loven, with a smile. 'This is what I so admire about this boy. He always thinks of others before himself.'

There was a pause while Mrs Loven tried to think of a solution.

'We only have one spare room,' she said, 'but I suppose Gerda could sleep there, while Torvil sleeps downstairs in the shop.'

'You have a shop?' said Torvil, beaming with delight.

'Then I suppose that's agreed,' said Mrs Loven, and the entire room erupted with laughter, cheers, and the sound of clapping.

'I don't get it,' said the reindeer. 'She just adopted both of you. Happy days, surely?'

But Torvil wasn't listening. He had turned from the window towards an imposing figure marching up the path, clouds of breath billowing from underneath his considerable moustache.

'Who's that?' whispered the reindeer.

'Mr Loven. The butcher,' said Torvil darkly.

'Freeze,' said the reindeer, its lips hardly moving. 'He mustn't see us.'

The two of them stood as still as statues, and watched as the butcher rang the bell at the orphanage door. Inside, Mrs Somby's ears pricked up and she ran to let him in. Mrs Loven, meanwhile, took Torvil and Gerda by the hand, and waited to greet him.

'Alva?' said the butcher to Mrs Loven in a gruff voice. 'What's going on?'

'Bryn,' said Mrs Loven. 'I want you to meet two new members of our family. Torvil and Gerda.'

'Two?' said the butcher. 'I agreed one.'

'Aren't they adorable?' said Mrs Loven.

'Expensive is what they are,' said the butcher.

'Children are like leeches,' he growled, and every child in the room felt the chill of his cold heart. 'All they do is take.'

'Oh, nonsense, Bryn,' said Mrs Loven, forcing a smile. 'I know you want a child just as much as I do.'

'Very well,' said the butcher. 'Girls make the best assistants. She comes. The boy stays here.' And with that, he turned on his heels and marched to the door.

'Wait!' called Mrs Loven and, grabbing Gerda's hand, rushed after him.

For a few moments, none of the children could quite believe what had happened. One by one, they all turned to look at Torvil, standing alone.

'That's decided, then,' said Mrs Somby, with a cruel smile. Leaning closer to teenage Torvil, she whispered, 'I told you not to trust that girl.'

'You see?' Torvil said to Rudolph. 'It was me she chose. But Gerda took my place.'

'Sssh,' said the reindeer. 'Listen.'

Gerda, Mrs Loven and the butcher were now at the orphanage door. Gerda was speaking firmly with the butcher, her fists clenched with determination.

'I'm not coming without Torvil,' she was saying. 'Either you adopt us both, or not at all.'

'Suits me,' said the butcher, heading for the gate.

'Gerda, please,' said Mrs Loven, lowering her voice. 'He doesn't mean it. It's just his way.'

'I'm not leaving Torvil,' said Gerda.

'You won't have to,' replied Mrs Loven. 'I can handle Bryn. You want the best for Torvil, don't you?'

Gerda frowned. 'Of course,' she said.

'Bryn will change his mind, you'll see. Then

'I'm not leaving Torvil,' said Gerda.

you'll both be out of this place.'

'Promise?' said Gerda.

'On my life,' said Mrs Loven. Taking Gerda by the hand, she began to follow the butcher along the path to the gate. As they walked, teenage Torvil appeared at the window, watching them go.

'See how heartbroken I am?' asked Torvil.

'You did hear that, didn't you?' asked the reindeer.

Torvil said nothing.

'Mrs Loven promised Gerda they would adopt you too. That's the only reason Gerda went with her.'

'Well, I don't know that, do I?' replied Torvil angrily. 'Look at me. Betrayed by my only friend.'

'It wasn't Gerda's fault.'

'You know whose fault it was?' snapped

Torvil, burning with shame. 'Mine. It was my fault for trying to do something good. Well, don't worry, I never made that mistake again.'

And without another word he stormed off through the grounds, towards the orphanage gates.

Chapter Thirteen

No sooner had Torvil reached the gates than the wind picked up again, flinging snowflakes so cold they burned his skin like hot pennies. Was the Copper Elf's magic working on him once again? If it was, he was determined to fight it. If he could run fast enough, he told himself, he might escape. But the harder he fought, the harder the winds blew. Putting one foot in front of the other became a colossal struggle, and he was soon exhausted to the point of collapse. Just when he felt he could bear it no more, the wind dropped, the snowflakes settled, and he found himself alone, standing in the middle of the town on a bright summer's morning.

Except this wasn't the town as he knew it now. This was the town of his youth. And there, right before him, was his shop; though instead of toys in the window, there were dusty second-hand books.

That's right, thought Torvil to himself. *This is the place as it was before I bought it. How did the old man who owned it ever make any money? No wonder I managed to get it so cheaply.*

The thought of the bargain price for which he had bought his little shop did wonders for Torvil's mood. Smiling to himself, he began a little daydream in which the dusty books with their measly penny prices were replaced by his expensive toys costing tens and hundreds of crowns. And he might have daydreamed for a good while longer had he not been awoken by a dreadful clatter coming from across the street.

His heart skipped a beat. There, dressed in a butcher's apron, was the lovely Gerda, rolling down the awning of the butcher's shop. Still a teenager, she appeared to him more beautiful than anyone wearing a hygienic hair net had any right to look.

He was about to call out her name when the butcher, standing at the open doorway, beat him to it.

'Gerda!'

'Yes, Father?,' she answered politely.

'Where are the sheep's eyes?'

'In the ice bucket, Father,' called Gerda, 'To keep them fresh.'

'Hmm,' said the butcher. 'They'd better be. Or they're coming out of your wages.'

Something about the moment seemed familiar to Torvil, and he was about to call to Gerda a second time when, yet again, someone else got there first.

'Gerda!'

A slender blond boy of little more than one hundred and forty was running down the street towards them. 'Gerda!' called the boy again, with great urgency. On his back was a rucksack, hung with various billy-cans and tin drinking cups, and as he ran they clattered and clanked like miniature cowbells. He was clearly in a very great hurry.

'Gerda, I've done it!' he said. 'I've run away from the orphanage!'

'What do you mean?' asked Gerda.

'Mrs Somby was at the gate, I dodged her. I'm free.'

'But . . . where will you go?'

'South,' said Torvil, struggling to get his breath. 'To seek my fortune. And I want you to come with me.'

'You know I can't do that,' said Gerda, leading him away from the open window of the butcher's shop. 'I wish I could, but I can't.'

'There you are,' said the reindeer, suddenly appearing beside Torvil. 'I've been looking for you all over.'

'Shhh! Keep your voice down,' whispered Torvil, and pointed to the two elves on the other side of the road.

'Oh, right,' said the reindeer, catching on. 'Sorry.'

'My mother is sick.' Gerda was saying. 'I can't leave her – she's really not well, Torvil.'

'Mother?' said young Torvil, scornfully. 'You've only been here two weeks!'

'They need me.'

'They need cheap labour.'

'I can't,' Gerda replied. 'They're all I've got.'

'But this is our chance,' pressed Torvil. 'Come with me. Please!'

There was a long pause, before Gerda slowly shook her head.

Young Torvil nodded and let go of Gerda's hand. Stooping to pick up his rucksack, he turned and began to walk in the direction he had come from. As she watched him go, Gerda's eyes welled with tears and she buried her face in her apron.

'She's crying,' said Torvil, amazed.

'Of course she's crying,' said the reindeer rolling his eyes. 'You just abandoned her.'

'I did not!' Torvil exclaimed. 'She abandoned me!'

'That's low self-esteem for you,' said the reindeer.

'Low what?' said Torvil.

'Long story,' said the reindeer. 'Got a touch of that myself. As my aunty always says, how can I expect other reindeer to respect me when I don't respect myself? No wonder they love to laugh and call me names.'

There was a pause while Torvil stared at him blankly. Then, seeing that his teenage self was already almost out of earshot, Torvil Christmas did something quite out of character; something no one had seen him do for a very long time. He began to run.

'We've got to stop him – I mean *me* – from leaving!' he cried, heading off across the street.

'Wait!' said the reindeer. 'This is the past, remember? You can't change it!'

'But if he leaves now it'll never be the same again,' said Torvil, already battling a rather painful stitch. 'When he comes back

121

they'll be strangers.'

It was too late. The wind was already picking up, and soon Torvil was once again lost in a blizzard of snow. He had no idea which way was forward or which way was back. As he stumbled off the path he found himself jogging down a large snowbank, then running, then sprinting, then sliding for some considerable distance on his stomach, before colliding head first with a young fir tree and knocking himself out.

Chapter Fourteen

'I think that bag of peas has warmed up. Could you fish them out of my boot?' said Father Christmas, jolting me from the story. I suddenly remembered where we were: on an enormous wooden sleigh, pulled by nine fully-grown reindeer, hurtling through the air about a kilometre off the ground.

Below us were the lights of a city, edged with black. 'Where are we?' I asked.

'Accra!' called Father Christmas. 'Capital of Ghana. They love Christmas here.'

The reindeer began to descend and we met a swell of warm, sweet-smelling air. Among the jumble of streets and buildings below us, I glimpsed a long, straight row of lights that I thought must be an airport runway.

'Is that where we're landing?' I asked.

'Goodness me, no,' said Father Christmas. 'I avoid planes. Freaks people out to see a flying reindeer through their window. We're going to land on the beach!'

Seconds later we buzzed over a wide freeway, jammed with traffic. Every lane was full of people, dancing, singing, and calling to one another from their cars.

'Where are they all going?' I asked.

'Nowhere!' said Father Christmas. 'They've been all over Ghana, visiting their relatives. On Christmas Eve, they all come home . . . and party!'

We skimmed a row of date palms, and below us I could see lush gardens and holiday-makers swimming in a turquoise pool. Then the reindeer banked a turn, and we were arcing out over the ink-blue ocean, as white waves raced to the shore.

'Hold tight!' called Father Christmas, as we kept turning and turning, until a ribbon of sandy beach opened out before us. Down plunged the reindeer, and I closed my eyes and gripped the rail tight, ready for anything. A few seconds later I realised that we weren't dropping any more, and the rails of the sleigh were sliding smoothly across the sand. We had landed!

'Is it safe?' I asked. 'There are so many people about, won't someone see us?'

'Ah,' said Father Christmas, smiling. 'This is where you find out my biggest secret. If you'd be so kind?'

I jumped down on to the sand and padded across to the other side of the sleigh, where Father Christmas was sitting. I crossed my fingers and held my hands in front of my chest, palms up, so as to make a foothold. Father Christmas placed his left boot in my hands, and swung his right leg around the back of my neck so that he was sitting on my shoulders. I passed the sack of presents up to him, he balanced it on my head, and we were on our way.

'Now then. "Won't someone see us?"' he said, repeating my question. 'Let me answer that question with another question. Have you ever seen a mouse?'

'Yes,' I replied. 'We've got two at my school. One is black, and the other one is white, brown and grey.'

'So you've seen a *pet* mouse,' said Father Christmas. 'What about a *house* mouse?'

'I don't think so,' I said.

'That's because pet mice are slow, and house mice are very, very fast,' said Father Christmas. 'Almost too fast to see.'

'Really?' I asked.

'Really,' said Father Christmas. 'You've probably got a dozen living in your skirting boards, but they move so quickly you've never noticed them. Now, let me ask you another question. Do you think *they* have ever seen *you*?'

'I don't know,' I said.

'Then I'll tell you,' said Father Christmas. 'They have. And how do you think you look to a house mouse? Fast or slow?'

I thought for a little while. 'Slow,' I replied.

'Really slow,' said Father Christmas. 'So slow as to be hardly moving.'

The beach was empty, but I could see a campfire glittering up ahead. Beyond it lay the yellow lights of the freeway, and the red and blue neon of the city. Suddenly I felt like the luckiest boy in the world: far from home, in an exciting country, sharing Father Christmas's deepest secrets.

'And let me ask you yet another question,' said Father Christmas. 'Before tonight, had you ever seen an elf?'

'No,' I said, shaking my head.

'And why do you think that might be?'

'Because they move too fast?' I guessed.

'Super, super fast,' he said, nodding. 'That's how I can get around the whole world in one night. If I hadn't got stuck in your chimney, and fallen into the fireplace, you'd never have seen me. I'd have been moving too fast. And here's the really amazing bit. Because I'm on your shoulders, you're moving superfast too. See?'

He stretched out his little hand and I looked

to where he was pointing. We had reached the campfire, and circled around it were a group of teenagers. I saw now that each of them was as still as stone, eyes unmoving, face frozen: one girl even had her eyes closed mid-blink. One of them had just thrown a cup of water at another, and the drops hung in the air like beads of glass.

'I don't understand,' I said.

'You're moving as fast as an elf now, and that's how humans look,' said Father Christmas. 'Which is why, if we are careful, no human will ever see us.'

I grinned a huge grin. One of the things I had been most worried about was getting caught, and ruining Christmas for good. Having super-speed really took the pressure off.

'Where's our first delivery?' I asked, keen to put myself to the test.

'Ah, yes,' said Father Christmas. 'One thing

you will quickly learn: things vary from country to country. Here, in Ghana, I don't come down the chimney. Instead, I leave the presents at church, and the children collect them in the morning. Which makes it nice and easy because I don't have to make lots of individual deliveries. That's our first drop off, right up ahead.'

'What, at the top of the hill?' I asked nervously. Father Christmas was surprisingly heavy for an elf, and the church he was pointing at was some way away.

'Don't worry,' he said. 'After this there's just ten thousand, five hundred and eighty-six to go.'

That sounded like a lot of carrying. I needed a distraction, fast.

'I don't suppose you could tell me what happens next in the story?' I asked.

'Excellent idea,' said Father Christmas. 'Where were we?'

'Torvil has just been knocked out again. By a fir tree.'

'So he has,' said Father Christmas. 'So he has.'

He continued to tell me the story as we delivered to the ten thousand, five hundred and eighty-seven churches in Ghana. And to all the children in Togo, Burkina Faso and the Côte d'Ivoire. And you'll know by now that this, pretty much word for word, is what he told me . . .

Chapter Fifteen

Torvil opened his eyes to find that, once again, he was lying on his back in the snow. Gingerly, he rolled over on to his side, then raised himself up on one elbow. On the edge of the forest, something caught his eye: the outline of a reindeer. A reindeer that looked very much like Rudolph.

'Well, don't just stand there,' Torvil bellowed. 'Help me up!'

But the animal simply gave him a long stare, then bounded off into the forest. Sitting up,

Torvil saw that he was at the foot of a tall, fully grown pine tree, and the snow around him was scattered with shards of broken wood.

Suddenly it dawned on him; he was back in the present. The broken-wood fragments were all that was left of the sled, now that the frightened huskies had dragged the rest of it off into the night. And the wild, red-nosed reindeer that had just run off into the forest was the same one he had so recently swerved to avoid.

He shook his head, and struggled to his feet. Now that he was back in the real world, it all seemed ridiculously far-fetched. A talking reindeer! Travelling through time! It was preposterous. The bump to his head had knocked him out and he had suffered a very vivid dream. There was nothing to do but put it all from his mind, and focus on the real task in front of him: getting safely home before he caught his death of cold in the forest. And yet . . .

Torvil frowned. Some of it had at least seemed real. The orphanage, for example. Of course he had no memory of being left there as a baby, but the scene he had witnessed did fit the facts he knew: he had been found in the early hours of Christmas Day and named Torvil Christmas as a result. It was true that he had been passed over for adoption in favour of Gerda and his feelings had been so hurt he thought he might never get over it. And it was most definitely true that he had run away from the orphanage . . .

It's extraordinary how the mind works, he thought to himself, as he trudged home along the forest path. His imagination, he decided, had ornamented a few small facts with an elaborate fantasy, like an oyster builds a pearl around a stubborn piece of grit. Had Gerda's eyes welled with tears the day he had left the town? He wished they had, and his dream had made it so. The truth . . . well, the truth might be different. Maybe she had cared for him, and maybe she hadn't; he would never know for sure. And what did it matter now, anyway? The past is the past, and you can never change it.

Thankfully, Torvil was now nearing his house on the hill, and with every step of the way he felt his breath come easier and his body relax. There were no gaudy Christmas decorations here: no striped candy canes on the gatepost, no evergreen wreaths on the door, and no coloured fairy lights on the large fir tree in the front garden. Everything was orderly, calm and dark. There were no neighbours to bother him either. Here, he could truly be alone.

He felt in his pocket for his door key, and as he did so, his fingers came across something hard and round. He fished it out, and placed it in his palm. It was the silver coin the Copper Elf had given him. He frowned. That made no sense: he had locked it away in the safe at the shop. Hadn't he? Maybe he had meant to put it in the safe, but stowed it in his pocket instead?

Torvil looked at again, carefully, trying to make sense of the elfin runes that were embossed on the back. Was that a reindeer, in the first of the three rows? What an extraordinary piece it was! Every time you examined it you noticed something new. It was worth a fortune, he was sure of that: the first elfin coins were collectors' items. What if he had lost it in the snow when he crashed the sled? Or if some rogue elf had taken it from his pocket while he lay unconscious, dreaming about the past? It wasn't worth thinking about. He must be much, much more careful in future.

One day, when he was old, he would take

it to a bank and exchange it for cash. Then he would go on a lovely summer holiday in Iceland, where he had heard it was often so warm that you could walk around in nothing more than a wool sweater. He grasped the coin tight. What a fortune he had been given! And how lucky was he, with no family or friends that he had to share it with?

It is indeed strange how the mind works. For no sooner had he convinced himself that his miserly ways were the path to true happiness when, from nowhere, a youthful memory flashed before him. There he was, a child again, handing Gerda his rag hedgehog, seeing her smile, and feeling joy in his heart. For a few seconds, he stood stock still, held in the moment. Then, with a shudder, it passed, and he dismissed it in the same way he would a gripe of stomach ache.

Chapter Sixteen

One of the challenges of living in such a large house, Torvil had long ago decided, was the expense. He'd wanted a big house, as he was sure it would be worth more money when it came to sell it, but in the meantime, he had to watch the pennies. The cost of lighting so many rooms, let alone heating them, would have been horrendous. Instead, Torvil had devised some clever methods of spending as little money as possible, methods he was extremely proud of.

Firstly, every time he went home, he used magic so as not to feel the cold. Every elf has a daily store of magic that they can choose to spend however they like. Most of Torvil's went on a sack that could hold an unlimited number of toys, to save on delivery costs at the toyshop, but he always used whatever was left over to make himself immune to temperature. That way he never needed to turn the heating on in his house, saving a fortune.

Secondly, he ate very little. If he felt hungry, he simply drank a pint of tap water. As a result he was unhealthily skinny, as well as being in a bad mood most of the time due to low blood sugar.

Finally – and most cleverly of all – he had constructed a web of ropes that ran from room to room so that he could find his way about in the dark, to avoid spending money on candles.

The only downside of living like this was that there wasn't all that much to do in the evenings, except go to bed. After all, there was no meal to cook, no one to talk to, no storybooks to read, or pleasure to be taken of any kind whatsoever. So, once he was safely inside the door, Torvil simply felt in the dark for the roughest of all the ropes, and followed it through the hall, up the main staircase, and into the master bedroom.

The bedroom, like the rest of the house, was pitch dark, but Torvil was used to it. Once inside, he followed a soft cotton rope to the bathroom, where he cleaned his teeth – making sure that he turned the tap off while he was brushing so that he didn't waste any water – and then followed a knotted linen rope to the bed. He felt in his pocket for the coin and placed it carefully under his pillow, where it couldn't get lost. Then he clambered in between the sheets, pulled up the bedclothes, and before he knew it was fast asleep.

Someone was whispering his name.

'*Torvillss! Torrrvillss!*'

For a few moments he lay in the dark, listening. Where had the voice come from?

The covers were halfway off the bed, as if he had been sleeping restlessly, and he pulled them back over his head, hoping to go to sleep again. Perhaps it had just been the wind in the trees.

No such luck.

'*Torvillss!*' came the voice again. '*Torvillssss!*'

Frowning, Torvil pulled back the shutter and pushed the window wide open. There, right in front of him, was the fir tree that had been growing in his front garden ever since he could remember, now lit by a high full moon. Only this time – unless he was very much mistaken – it was talking to him.

'There you are!' it hissed, and as it spoke, smatterings of fresh snow fell from its branches, revealing the outline of eyelashes, a nose and a mouth. 'Come on, or we'll be late!'

'Late?' said Torvil in return, wondering if he might still be dreaming. 'Late for what?'

'Late for, you know, er . . . your mate . . . little fellow?' said the tree, gesturing with one of its branches. 'Pointy hat . . . fingers . . . wispy, er . . . beard . . .'

'Steinar?' said Torvil.

'That's the one!' said the tree.

'But I can't be late for Steinar,' said Torvil. 'He works for me. That's the beauty of being an employer. I come and go as I please, but if he's a minute late I dock his wages. In any case, he's

'Come on, or we'll be late.'

not due for another . . .' Torvil's voice trailed off as he looked at his bedside clock. 'Good gracious. Five hours.'

'Ah,' said the fir tree, pulling up one of its roots. 'You think we're going to the . . . you know, the place. Children . . . wheels . . . windows . . . the, umm . . .'

'Toyshop?' offered Torvil.

'That's it! The toyshop.' The tree breathed a sigh of relief that it had finally found the right word. 'Well, we're not!'

'Too right we're not,' said Torvil. 'Because I'm going back to bed.'

'Oh,' said the fir tree, with an expression of surprise. 'Okay. Well, if you're not bothered about the spell . . .'

'What spell?' said Torvil warily.

'You know,' said the tree. 'The one the, er, the whatsit, put on you . . . little chap, red hair

145

'. . . unusually large teeth . . .'

'The Copper Elf?' asked Torvil.

'It's very annoying when people do that,' huffed the tree. 'As I was just about to say – before I was so rudely interrupted – the spell the Copper Elf put on you.'

'And what would you know about that?' asked Torvil.

'Me?' said the tree, astonished. 'Well, let me think. Because I'm the second of your three visitors? Come to save you from misery? But what do I know? I'm just a talking Christmas tree.'

'I'm sorry,' said Torvil. 'I think you must have got me mixed up with someone. I'm not miserable. I'm one of the richest elves in town. And no one said anything to me about three visitors. No offence, but you could be anybody. Or anything. A hill-daemon, maybe, or a water-warlock, shape-changing to trick me. And if you think I'm about to follow you into the woods at this time of night you are very much mistaken. I mean, really, I've never heard such nonsense!'

'Nonsense, is it?' asked the tree, pulling up the last of its roots. 'Check the whatsit . . . on the coin . . . the inscription!' And, with that, it stumbled off across the garden, scattering soil as it went.

Torvil reached under his pillow, and held the coin up to the moonlight. There were three rows of runes on the back. In the first there was a reindeer, just as there had been the last time he looked. And in the second, he now saw something that looked very like a fir tree.

'Wait!' called Torvil.

But the fir tree did nothing of the sort.

Chapter Seventeen

Seconds later, Torvil was at his own front door, pulling on his leather boots. Unfortunately, because he was wearing his very thickest bed socks, he had great difficulty getting the boots on properly, and by the time he made it outside, the tree was nowhere to be seen. Huffing and puffing with the inconvenience of it all, Torvil snatched a walking cane from the pot, and followed the tree's muddy trail across the lawn and through the gate at the far end of the garden.

Much to his surprise, when he reached the lane on the other side of the gate, it too was empty. Fir trees, it turned out, are nimbler than you'd think. Luckily, its roots were shedding soil, and Torvil could see that after following the icy road for a few hundred metres, the tree had veered off sharply to the left. In fact, there it was now, stomping towards the brow of the hill, heading for the town.

Torvil gave chase, and soon found himself standing flush-faced on the hill top, looking out across the moonlit valley. Below him, to the right, was the close-packed West Village where he had his shop, and beyond that lay the spacious homes and gardens of the rich elves. To the left was the disused shoe factory and the closely packed cottages of the East Village. That was the part of town where the poor elves lived and, sure enough, way below him, there was the fir tree, pushing its way through the edge of the forest and into an alleyway.

Before he knew it, Torvil was yomping down the mountainside, and rapidly gaining on the tree. 'Wait!' he called. 'Wait!' But if anything, the tree put on a burst of speed, and by the time Torvil reached the alleyway it had vanished. Its roots had stopped dropping soil, and the snow on the ground was too hard to show scuff marks. Which way had it gone?

Torvil never visited this part of town; there were fences in need of repair, overflowing rubbish bins, and battered old sleighs up on bricks. Trusting to luck, he wove his way through the tiny cobbled streets, glancing this way and that, looking for any sign that might lead him to the tree. On a couple of occasions he thought he glimpsed it ahead as it ducked down an alley or pitter-pattered down a back lane. But try as he might, he just couldn't keep up. And then, horror of horrors, he realised it had given him the slip.

He was just turning towards home when a beam of light illuminated the wall at the end of a particularly narrow lane. And there, in silhouette, was the fir tree.

The tree stood at the bright window of the tiniest shack in the whole of the East Village. And what a shack it was! Its eaves were freshly painted in the traditional colours of red, green and cobalt blue, and its tiny front yard glittered with wind chimes and potted shrubs. On the door was a homemade wreath of ivy, wild rosemary and red forest berries, and there were paper chains hanging from beneath the windows.

'There you are!' said Torvil with relief.

'Shhhh!' said the tree. 'They've just

woken up.'

'Who has?' said Torvil.

'What? You don't know who lives here?' said the tree.

'Of course not,' said Torvil. 'This is the East Village, where the poor elves live. As I keep trying to tell you, I'm rich.'

'In that case,' said the tree, giving him a stern look, 'come and take a, er . . . a, whatsit . . . look.'

Torvil gave a little snort, which he often did when people said something he didn't much approve of, but curiosity got the better of him, and he stepped forward to gaze through the window. Inside, a pretty female elf with brown hair was putting the finishing touches to one of the smallest, spindliest Christmas trees he had ever seen.

'Wow,' said Torvil. 'That is one tiny tree.

Thank you for the experience.'

The tree turned to look at him, as if it didn't quite understand what he was saying.

'That's what we've come to see, right?' asked Torvil. 'The smallest Christmas tree in the world. That's some serious crafting, right there. I mean, those baubles are minute.'

'At least their tree has, you know, the things that hang down . . .'

'Decorations?'

'Oh, so you *do* know what they are,' said the fir tree pointedly. 'Then how come you've never bought me so much as a strand of tinsel?'

Not quite knowing what to say, Torvil simply shrugged his shoulders.

'Anyway,' said the tree. 'That's not why we're here. Keep . . . you know . . . thingy . . . watching.' As the tree spoke, a familiar figure entered, carrying half a dozen juicy sausages on a large wooden platter.

'Steinar!' said Torvil, shocked to see his chief toymaker awake so early and in so happy a mood.

'Tah dah!' said Steinar, by way of a fanfare, as he set the sausages down on the tiny table. On a serving dish sat a small roast potato and two thin carrots, and next to that a jug of watery-looking gravy. And yet despite it being such a modest meal, the female elf – who Torvil now realised must be Freya, Steinar's wife – applauded, and Steinar took a bow.

'What on earth are they doing?' asked Torvil in surprise.

'Having their Christmas dinner,' replied the tree.

'But it's the middle of the night!' said Torvil.

'Indeed it is,' said the tree, nodding its upper branches. 'You wouldn't give him the, you know, time off. So if they want to spend

Christmas together they have to do it now.'

'Right,' said Torvil quietly. 'I see.'

Inside, Steinar's wife pointed to the clock and said something to Steinar, who nodded, and took a medicine bottle from the shelf. He opened a door, revealing a staircase, and started to climb it to the floor above.

'Where's he going?' asked Torvil.

'Why don't you find out?' asked the tree. 'Come on, up you come.'

Chapter Eighteen

Fir trees aren't the easiest of things to climb, and it took a moment or two for Torvil to work out that he had to push his way inside the tree, out of the way of its needles, so that he could get a foothold in the more spacious region where its branches met its trunk. Hand over hand he climbed, until he found his head emerging from between its spindly upper branches.

He was now at the top of the house, looking in through an open window into a bedroom.

The room was dark, but the moon was easily bright enough for Torvil to see that there was a child in the bed, tucked up warmly and sleeping soundly. The bedroom door opened, and in crept Steinar, lighting the way with a candle. He sat beside the bed and whispered gently.

'Kiti. Wake up, Kiti. It's Christmas.'

'Daddy!' said Kiti, opening first one eye and then the other. 'Happy Christmas!'

'Happy Christmas!' said Steinar, pouring a spoonful of medicine. 'We've got a slap-up roast dinner downstairs and we thought you might like to join us?'

'Really?' said Kiti, wincing as she swallowed. 'What are we having?'

'Sausages,' said Steinar.

'Lucky me!' said Kiti. 'Lucky *us*!'

'I know,' said Steinar. 'But I do have something rather sad to tell you. I know you wanted a bicycle for Christmas . . .'

'Oh, not really, Daddy,' said Kiti. 'I only said that because Mummy asked me what I would wish for if I could have anything at all.'

'Oh, Kitty,' said Steinar, his eyes moistening with tears. 'I'm afraid we couldn't afford one. But I did make you this . . .' And Steinar handed Kiti a small present, wrapped in brown paper.

'Thank you, Daddy!' said Kiti, 'Thank you so much!' and she tore off the paper to reveal a tiny bicycle carved from wood.

'It's perfect!' said Kiti, throwing her arms around his neck.

'Come on, time for that dinner,' said Steinar, wiping away a stubborn tear, and he and Kiti began to make their way down the narrow staircase, the candlelight casting both their shadows on the stairwell, then shuttering into darkness as the door closed downstairs.

He and Kiti began to make their way down the narrow staircase.

Torvil, his head still poking out from the upper branches of the tree, nodded thoughtfully.

'Lovely girl, that, erm . . . Kiti, isn't she?' said the tree. 'You could tell she was so . . . disappointed, you know, about the bike. But did she show it? No.'

'Well, there's always next year,' said Torvil, feeling slightly uncomfortable.

'Ah,' said the tree. 'You're feeling guilty.'

'Excuse me?' said Torvil.

'Well, it's your fault, isn't it?' said the tree.

'My fault?' said Torvil. 'What's my fault?'

'It's your . . . whatsername, isn't it?' said the tree. 'Meanness. You don't pay Steinar enough, don't give him days off. You've ruined their Christmas, haven't you?'

'Woah, woah, woah,' said Torvil. 'Stop right there. Did I close the shoe factory? Did I devalue the crown? At least Steinar has a job. There are

161

plenty of elves around here who would love to be in his position, let me tell you.'

'Wow,' said the tree. 'You really do feel . . . whatsit . . . guilty.'

'No!' said Torvil, stamping his foot. 'No, no, no, no, no! I'm not having you blame this on me!' At which point the branch that he was standing on snapped, and he immediately began to fall.

Chapter Nineteen

'ang on,' said Father Christmas in a voice that told me this wasn't part of the story. 'I need to concentrate for this bit.'

I had been so wrapped up in Torvil and little Kiti, I had failed to notice the night had somehow turned to day. A few minutes before, we had taken off from the Cape, at the very tip of Africa, where the Atlantic meets the Pacific, heading due south. We were now descending through bright cloud, and I saw that tiny ice crystals had begun to form on my dressing gown. That could only mean one thing: we were near the South Pole.

'There!' said Father Christmas, as the final wisps curled from view. 'Look! The Antarctic coast!'

The clouds parted, and I was almost blinded by the most dazzling sunshine. Before us was a colossal field of icebergs, floating like sugar lumps in the dark-blue ocean. I looked to where Father Christmas was pointing and I could just about make out a ribbon of grey pebble beach, crowned by a wall of ice.

Seconds later, the cliffs rushed up to meet us, and everywhere I looked, all I could see was snow. We were flying over Antarctica! A causeway of dark mountain peaks stretched out in front of us, surrounded on either side by an ocean of glimmering white.

'See?' shouted Father Christmas. 'The Transantarctic Mountains. They lead all the way to the South Pole.'

'I don't understand,' I shouted back. 'Why is the sun shining?'

'Ah,' said Father Christmas, clearly pleased that I had asked. 'Because it's summer.'

'I understand,' I said, although I didn't.

'When it's winter at the North Pole, it's summer here,' said Father Christmas. 'The sun shines for the whole of Christmas.'

'But there can't be any children at the South Pole,' I said.

'Usually there aren't,' said Father Christmas. 'But this year's different. See down there?' I nodded. 'That is a research station. It's full of scientists, and one of them . . . well, you'll see in a minute. Look out!'

'*Yah!*' he bellowed, and gave the reins an

authoritative shake.

'Will you please stop doing that?' called Rudolph, from way up in front. 'I find it mildly condescending!'

'Sorry!' called out Father Christmas.

'Come on, team!' shouted Rudolph, and the reindeer began to take the full weight of the sleigh, pulling us up into a steep climb. Doing my best not to look scared, I fumbled around on the seat to see if there might be anything resembling a safety harness. There wasn't. We were now slowing to a halt, as if at the very top of a giant rollercoaster, and sure enough, Father Christmas put his hands in the air.

'Woohoo!' he called.

'Woohoo!' I shouted, and stuck my hands in the air too.

The rest is a bit of a blur. One minute I was staring at the sky, and the next at the ground, while Rudolph and the other reindeer galloped at full tilt. The wind was so fierce it was almost impossible to open my eyes, although once I did, I immediately wished I hadn't. We were coming up much too fast on a large rectangular grey building, surrounded by a brightly coloured jumble of huts and tents.

It wasn't going to be much of a Christmas present, I thought to myself, if we ended up flattening the whole camp.

'Is this safe?' I called out to Father Christmas.

'Goodness me, no,' he shouted. 'It's absolute idiocy! But that's what makes it fun!'

Suddenly, there was a jolt and Father Christmas and I were flung into the footwell.

'AAARGH!' Father Christmas cried, and I sensed that this wasn't exactly soothing his swollen ankle.

We had landed. The sleigh was still in one

piece, but we were careering across the ice so fast that it felt like we might never stop.

'Pull on the reins!' I called to Father Christmas.

'You pull on the reins!' he called out, stuffing them into my hands.

'STOP!' I shouted to the reindeer, and I stood up, and pulled as hard as I could.

Gradually, the pack slowed from a gallop to an ever-so-slightly slower gallop, then to a canter, and finally drew to a halt just a metre or so from a black-and-white pole with a shiny sphere on top.

'Blimey,' said Rudolph. 'We nearly broke the South Pole.'

Chapter Twenty

'**R**ight!' said Father Christmas. 'No time to lose.'

'Absolutely,' I said, and jumped down from the sleigh. Unfortunately I was still dressed in my night clothes, and I discovered that there is very good reason you never see a polar explorer in cotton pyjamas, slippers and a dressing gown. The South Pole is *cold*. A light breeze skipped across the snow to greet us, and I felt like I had been pricked by a thousand tiny burning needles. Then Father Christmas hopped on to my shoulders and, suddenly, it was as if I was in a bubble. The ice, the snow, the bitter air: none of it could touch me.

'I'm . . . I'm not cold any more! What's happened?' I asked Father Christmas.

'What part of *magic* don't you understand?' said Father Christmas, tousling my hair to show that he was teasing. 'I'm an elf, and my magic means I don't feel the cold. And while I'm on your shoulders, neither do you.'

He was right! It didn't matter how bitterly the wind blew, I was as cosy as if I were at home in my nice warm bed.

'Now, then,' said Father Christmas. 'I think that's our target, over there.'

Tents are easier to get into than houses, and soon we were standing in the yellow glow of a large circular canvas dome, surrounded by a wall of whiteboards, each of which was inscribed with all sorts of diagrams and important-looking mathematics. In the middle of the floor was a crib, draped with gauze and hung with fairy lights. Standing next to it was a mother holding a baby in her arms, her eyes wide in a loving gaze, frozen as still as a statue.

'As I say, I don't usually deliver to the South Pole,' said Father Christmas. 'But then I heard that Miss Bellwater here had a new arrival.'

I looked again at the lady and her baby, then at the wonderful drawings and equations on the walls around us.

'But what are all these diagrams?' I asked. One day, when I grew up, I thought I might like to write mathematics and make complicated pictures like these.

'Miss Bellwater's a scientist,' replied Father Christmas. 'She's working on something truly incredible. It's the world's biggest telescope, and it's made entirely from ice.'

'Where is it?' I asked secretly hoping we might have time to take a look.

'The telescope? You're standing on it,' said Father Christmas. 'It's right under your feet, in fact, it's under the entire South Pole. The ice here is so pure that they can use it to detect a very special kind of particle, called a neutrino. Neutrinos are everywhere, but it's very hard to see them.'

'A bit like you,' I said.

'Yes, I suppose so,' said Father Christmas. 'You can tell where a neutrino has been, because when it hits a water molecule, it sends out a tiny beam of light. And you can tell when I've been, because I leave at least one present. Which is exactly what I'm going to do now.'

In one corner of the tent was a little silver Christmas tree made of tinsel, and I walked towards it with Father Christmas on my shoulders.

'Okay,' said Father Christmas. 'Hand me the sack.'

'What sack?' I asked.

'Good one,' said Father Christmas. 'I like a boy with a sense of humour. The sack with all the presents in it.'

'Um . . . I haven't got it,' I said.

'I specifically asked you to bring it,' said Father Christmas.

'No, you didn't,' I replied, before I quite remembered to whom I was talking. 'It must be on the sleigh,' I said, more politely. 'Shall I go and fetch it?'

'No time,' said Father Christmas, glancing at his watch. 'It's nearly two a.m. and we haven't done North and South America yet. Sorry, baby Sean.'

I felt very bad. We couldn't leave Sean without giving him a present! Everyone should always have a special first present from Father Christmas. And that's when I had an idea . . .

'I could give him Mr Bodecca?' I suggested.

'Mr Who?' asked Father Christmas.

'Here,' I said, and produced my cuddly rabbit from my dressing-gown pocket. He had been my first gift from Father Christmas and my best friend ever since. I always slept with him by my side.

'Ah, so that's what you called him,' said Father Christmas. 'Hello, Mr Bodecca. I remember you. But, Jackson . . . are you sure?'

'Definitely,' I said. 'It'll be like when Torvil gave Gerda his rag hedgehog.'

'Won't you miss him?' said Father Christmas.

'A lot,' I said. 'But that's better than Sean not having a present.'

'Could you put me down for a minute?' asked Father Christmas, and I set him next to the tree.

Father Christmas frowned, and I wondered for a moment if he might be cross. Then he took off his glasses, and rubbed his eyes. After a few moments, he put his glasses back on, and I saw there was a tear on his cheek.

'You're a good boy,' he said in a gruff voice, and placed Mr Bodecca beside the little Christmas tree. 'High-five,' he said, and I slapped my hand against his red velvet glove.

Moments later, Father Christmas was back on my shoulders, and a strong wind was gusting at my back.

'As a reward, maybe you'd like to hear a bit more of the story?' asked Father Christmas. 'I can tell it to you while we make our deliveries in South America.'

'I was hoping you might say that,' I replied.

The wind was so strong that I was now jogging against my will.

'Where were we again?'

'Torvil has visited the past, and now the present,' I said. 'When we last saw him, he was falling through the branches of the Christmas tree.'

'So he was,' replied Father Christmas. 'So he was.'

And this . . . well, this is exactly what he told me.

Chapter Twenty-One

Down fell Torvil, bouncing from branch to branch, sometimes landing on his bottom, sometimes on his belly, and once or twice on his chin, which was really rather painful indeed. Now and then he tried to grasp a branch in order to slow his descent, and each time he did so there was a splintering sound and it came away in his hand. Just when it seemed that he would continue being buffeted and tuffeted for ever, he came to an abrupt halt on something very hard and flat.

It took Torvil a few seconds to realise that the hard and flat thing in question was his own bedroom floor, and that the branches he had thought he was tangled up in were actually his bedclothes. Opening his eyes, he ran a swift check to see if any of his bones were broken, but it seemed – miracle of miracles – that he was all in one piece. He looked at the clock on his bedside table; it was a little after four in the morning. There was no point trying to get back to sleep, so he might as well head into work. He could get a head-start on that stocktake. But, first, there was something he needed to check . . .

Torvil took a deep breath, walked to the window, and pulled back the shutters. To his great relief, there in the front garden, swaying in the wind, was the same old fir tree. There were no signs of a muddy trail or any broken branches. So there it was: proof it had all been a dream. There had been no talking reindeer, no talking tree, no early Christmas feast at Steinar's house, and no tiny bicycle for Steinar's daughter, Kiti. And since none of those things had happened, he decided, there was no need whatsoever for him to feel guilty.

With that settled in his mind, Torvil emerged from his front door in what felt like a jolly mood. And he felt even jollier when he realised he was just in time to catch one of the few passenger sleighs that day. What a treat lay ahead: a whole day of going through all the items of stock in the toyshop, together with their prices, to calculate the year's profits, without being bothered by pesky customers. The very thought made him chuckle with glee.

Torvil's house was last on the forest road, and usually he had the whole sleigh to himself until they reached the edges of town. On this particular morning, however, just as they reached the densest part of the forest, a dark figure stepped out from the trees and into the path. The driver pulled to a halt and an elderly lady climbed aboard.

A ragged black shawl covered her head and shoulders, and she was very stooped, so it was impossible to see her face. She was feeling her way with a long walking stick, and Torvil quickly realised that she must be blind. For the briefest of moments, he felt the urge to help her, but managed to overcome it. She was probably a beggar, he told himself, and only pretended to be blind to make people feel sorry for her. Well, he wouldn't give her a penny!

'Good morning,' said the old lady politely, as she staggered and swayed up the aisle. 'Is there a spare seat here, by any chance?' Of course, with the rest of the sleigh empty, there was no one to answer her, so each time she simply shrugged and moved on. 'Good morning,' she said again. 'Is there a spare seat by any chance?'

Torvil folded his arms and crossed his legs and pretended to be fascinated by the passing scenery. And as he did so, the Copper Elf's coin fell out of his pocket and rolled on to the floor.

The old lady's eyesight might have been poor, but her hearing was excellent, and with one swift movement of her walking stick she pinned the coin to a floorboard. Then, steadying herself with one hand, she bent to pick it up.

'I'm so sorry,' said Torvil quickly. 'That belongs to me.'

The old lady frowned. 'Do I know you, sir?' she asked.

'I don't think so,' said Torvil.

'Your voice . . . it sounds familiar.'

'I have a shop in town,' said Torvil. 'Perhaps you are a lover of high-quality toys?'

'No,' said the old lady, shaking her head. 'That's not it. What's your name, if you don't mind my asking?'

'Torvil.'

'And your surname?' said the old lady.

'Christmas. Torvil Christmas.'

'Ah,' said the old lady, pulling back her shawl. 'This really is a very unusual coin,' she said, examining it with her fingertips. 'Is that a reindeer I can feel there?'

'Yes, yes, I think that is a reindeer,' said Torvil, wishing she would give the coin back. It was extremely valuable, after all.

'And next to it . . . is that a fir tree?'

'Possibly,' said Torvil.

'And what's this strange creature . . . a bear?'

'Creature?' asked Torvil.

'There's something around its neck,' said the old lady. 'A scarf, maybe?'

'That's funny,' said Torvil. 'I never noticed that before. Let me see. Well . . . I think that's a snowman.'

'A penguin, perhaps?'

'I SAID, I THINK IT'S A SNOWMAN,' said Torvil loudly, and tried to take the coin in his grasp. But the old lady held on to it firmly and drew him close.

'Don't you recognise me?' she said in a low voice.

'I think you must have me confused with someone else,' said Torvil, slightly alarmed.

'I don't think so. I would never forget you, Torvil Christmas. I named you, after all.'

For a few seconds, Torvil's face was as blank as a field of fresh snow. And then . . .

'Miss Turi?' he asked.

He could see it now: her face might be wrinkled, but those were quite definitely Miss Turi's bright blue eyes.

'How is Gerda?' she asked. 'Are you two still in touch?'

'Umm . . .'

'Of course you are. How could you not be?'

Torvil gave a little awkward laugh.

'What a fine jacket,' she said, feeling the collar of his red velvet suit. 'You must be rich.'

'Not really,' said Torvil awkwardly.

'Tell me,' she said. 'Did you ever bring presents to the children at the orphanage, like you said you would?'

'I . . . I . . .' said Torvil, but no other words came out.

'I thought so,' she replied. 'You always were such a lovely boy.'

Smiling, she placed the coin in Torvil's gloved

palm and closed his fingers around it. The driver was slowing for the next stop and Torvil saw that they were approaching the orphanage. By the time he looked back, the old lady was halfway down the aisle.

'Miss Turi!' he called, as she made her way towards the front of the sleigh. He needed to talk to her, to prove to himself that the Torvil she had known, the kinder, thoughtful Torvil, was still there, deep inside him. 'Please! Wait!'

But the old lady didn't seem to hear him. They were still a good few kilometres from town, and there would be no other sleigh for at least an hour, but Torvil didn't think twice: as quickly as he could, he gathered up his things and headed after her.

Chapter Twenty-Two

There were patches of fog on the roadside, and Torvil could see no sign of the old lady. But as the sleigh pulled away, he caught a glimpse of her some way off, by the orphanage gates.

'Miss Turi!' he called. 'Miss Turi!'

And then the strangest thing happened: she pulled back her shawl, and turned towards him. But instead of the kindly face of Miss Turi, Torvil saw the low forehead, hooked nose and fierce green eyes of the Copper Elf. Or, at least, he thought he did. Because the next instant, a blanket of fog descended, burying him in white.

Could it be that the reindeer and the fir tree had been real, after all? There were three creatures on the coin – what if there was still another visit to come?

'Hello!' Torvil called nervously. He was answered only by silence. The fog was so thick that when he stretched his arms, he could barely make out his own red gloves. Now he knew who his third visitor would be: a snowman. That didn't sound too scary. So why did he feel so uneasy?

The best course of action, he decided, was to head for the town. If he could find the gates of the orphanage, then he might be able to point himself in the right direction. When he had glimpsed Miss Turi – or was it the Copper Elf? – the gates had been only forty paces or so away.

Once he found the gates, he could find the path, and once he found the path, he could find the town.

The problem was that he had no idea in which direction the gates might lie. After thinking for a moment, he hit upon a rather ingenious plan. Taking off his gloves, he scooped up two large handfuls of snow, and began to pack them together into a snowball. He put his gloves back on and rolled the snowball around in the fresh snow until it was the size of a football. That, he decided, would make the perfect marker.

Standing with his back to the snowball, he took exactly forty steps forward. There was no sign of the gate, so he about-turned, and counted forty steps back. To his great joy, there was the snowball, exactly where he had left it. It was somewhat larger than he remembered: more the size of a boulder than a football, but that must be his mind playing tricks in the fog. No matter; his plan was working. He shuffled around the snow-boulder so that he was facing a new, unexplored direction, and set off once again to take forty paces.

The fog was even thicker now, and after forty steps, when he held his arms in front of his face he couldn't see further than his elbow. He frowned. The gates might be as close as a single step away, and he would never know. What was he to do? No kind of weather lasts for ever, and eventually the fog would surely lift, but for the time being it was all rather unsettling. At least he had his boulder for comfort, he decided, and about-turned to take forty steps back.

'One, two, three . . .' he counted out loud, taking care to make sure each step was the same size as the last, so that he might end up in the correct place. 'Four, five, six . . .'

He stopped. The fog began to rapidly disappear, as a towering shape appeared in the whiteness: a snowball so vast that if Torvil had stretched his arms wide, he couldn't have hoped to outsize it. Pressed into the side of it, way above his head, were three stone boulders, each the size of a small cottage. 'Seven, eight, nine . . .' he said in a flat voice, unable to believe what his eyes were telling him, then, 'ten,' in a half-whisper, as he took his final hesitant step. Looking up, he saw the dark outline of a giant carrot, silhouetted against the sky. There was no mistaking it: he was standing at the feet of the most enormous snowman the world had ever seen.

Chapter Twenty-Three

Torvil was just thinking that the forest that had seemed so unappealing to him was perhaps not so dark and dangerous, after all, and that it might even be a good place to hide from a giant snowman, when he heard a low rumbling and cracking sound that filled him with dread. He had heard something similar once before, shortly before an avalanche, and he immediately felt the impulse to run. Looking up, he wished that he had, because the creature was starting to move.

Snow began to fall in torrents, and Torvil raised his arms to protect himself. When he looked up again, he saw that the snowman's entire head had loomed into view, and was now clearly visible as a second distant summit beyond the unimaginable heights of its belly. Above its colossal carrot nose, it had two huge black boulders for eyes, and around its neck was an enormous multi-coloured scarf.

'And where might you be going?' boomed the snowman, with a predictably terrifying voice.

'To the town?' said Torvil, with as much confidence as he could muster.

'Speak up!' bellowed the snowman.

'To the town, sir. I own a humble toyshop,' quaked Torvil.

'Not any more, you don't.'

'Don't I?' said Torvil, trying not to sound like he knew better. He knew very little about giant snowmen, but he had a feeling they didn't particularly like being corrected by teeny tiny elves. 'It . . . it was there yesterday.'

'No, it wasn't,' said the snowman. 'But then, we are a thousand years in the future.'

Torvil nodded. If someone had stopped him in the street a couple of days before and told him that a giant snowman was about to time-travel him forward an entire millennium, he would have thought they were in need of therapy. But somehow, coming as it did after an adventure into the past with a red-nosed reindeer, and a midnight journey with a talking tree, it really didn't seem that strange. In fact, it sort of made sense: past, present, future. Now he had the full set.

'Come,' said the snowman. 'Let's walk.'

Torvil was about to say that he was fine where he was, thank you very much, when down came

Down came an enormous wooden finger and thumb...

an enormous wooden finger and thumb and plucked him by the hood of his red velvet jacket. Although terrifying, it was oddly thrilling, and Torvil wondered for a moment if this jolt of excitement was what all helpless animals felt in the brief seconds before they were swallowed whole by a killer whale, or torn limb from limb by a polar bear.

Within mere seconds Torvil was higher than the treetops, and even merer seconds after that he was higher than the birds. The snowman set him upon its shoulder, and began taking great strides over the forest, in much the same way that a tall elf might pick his way through long summer grass. Torvil didn't like heights – in fact, he often asked Steinar to fetch the toys from the top shelf – but this was different: he was so high up that he felt like he was in another world.

In a few short strides the giant reached the lip of the valley, and began crashing down the other side towards the town. As he soared above the close-packed streets and cottages of the East Village, it was immediately apparent to Torvil that something was very wrong indeed. Street after street was deserted, and there were no lights in any of the windows. The place was like a ghost town.

'Where is everyone?' he shouted.

'Gone,' said the snowman.

'Gone where?'

'Iceland, some of them. Greenland. Canada. Quite a few in Canada, actually. They're attracted by the maple syrup. But there's no magic any more. They've all got steady jobs. Dry cleaning, that's quite popular. A lot of them work for eBay. I did hear of one elf that became a newsreader in Indonesia, though by and large they keep out of sight.'

'But this is our home,' said Torvil.

'Well, it was all right for you, wasn't it? The rest of them . . . they had nothing.'

'Now, hang on,' said Torvil. 'I didn't start out with a silver spoon in my mouth, you know. I worked hard to build a— *Woooaaahh*!'

Once again, the giant grabbed Torvil by the hood, and lifted him through the air before setting him down outside a familiar-looking shop. Its windows were boarded, and its sign was faded, but it was recognisable all the same. On the door was a weathered notice which read: *Closing-down Sale*.

'. . . build a business,' finished Torvil quietly.

For a few moments he stood, staring at his old toyshop, then slowly turned to look up at the snowman.

'What happened?'

'Take a look around . . .' The snowman waved his arm in the general direction of the empty town, causing a tiny flurry of snow. 'Does this look like a good location for a high-end toyshop?'

'I went bust,' said Torvil mournfully.

'No,' said the snowman.

'No?' echoed Torvil.

'No,' repeated the snowman. 'You got out.'

'How?'

'You sold to a big company,' said the snowman. 'There are one thousand, four hundred and forty-four of these Torvil toyshops now, spread right across the world, copied down to the last detail. And all of them pay you money.'

'*Pay* me?' asked Torvil. 'As in, the present tense? I'm still living?'

'You *exist*,' said the snowman. 'I wouldn't say you were *living*.'

'How much do they pay me?' said Torvil.

'A lot,' said the snowman. 'You are rich beyond your wildest dreams.'

'Are you serious?'

'You don't believe me?' said the snowman. 'Come and see.'

Chapter Twenty-Four

I t was an odd thing, but Torvil actually found himself enjoying the journey back across the town. He was feeling less wary of the snowman now, and it was thrilling to see the world from such a great height. Besides, he was delighted at the rosiness of his future. He was rich! All those early mornings, all those arguments with suppliers, all those wranglings over employees' pay – it had all been worth it. He had made something of himself, and people had to take notice. He was a success.

Torvil was expecting the giant snowman to set him down outside his old familiar farmhouse, so for a few moments after his feet touched the ground he struggled to recognise where he was. Then everything shifted into place, and he realised he was standing outside the orphanage instead.

Once again, though, it looked different. The garden had been replaced with a beautiful limestone pebble path circling two enormous shallow pools, each the size of small lake, complete with dancing fountains and lights. Standing either side of the freshly painted front door were two neat bay trees, and immediately either side each of those were giant torches, hurling hot yellow flames high into the cold night air.

'Wow,' said Torvil. 'They've really spruced the old place up, eh?'

To his left, through the ground-floor window, the refectory was barely recognisable: its walls were hung with expensive-looking early elfin rugs, restored battle weapons and breastplates from ancient suits of armour and, standing where the rough old wooden trestle table used to be, was a giant stuffed polar bear. To his right, the matron's threadbare office was decorated in an oriental theme, complete with lanterns, screens, and dark lacquered wooden walls. Whatever the orphanage budget might be these days, it clearly stretched to some pretty punchy interior design.

'Wait a minute . . .' said Torvil. 'Don't tell me I did this?'

'Oh, yes,' said the snowman.

'Bit extravagant,' said Torvil, pretending to be cross but secretly feeling rather proud. 'This must be the most lavish orphanage in the entire

North Pole! Must have gone soft in my old age, but what can I say? The place meant a lot to me. After all, if they hadn't taken me in . . . Rich people. *Cuh.* What are we like? We scrimp and save to build up a fortune, then we just give it all away. I dare say the orphans are delighted.'

'Orphan,' said the snowman, emphasising the 'n'.

'Only one?' said Torvil. 'I bet he can't believe his luck.'

'You'd have to ask him,' said the snowman, and before he could protest, Torvil felt cold snow on his neck as he was hoisted upwards by the scruff of his red velvet jacket. Speeding towards the windows of the dormitory, he was fully expecting to find the room beyond utterly transformed. Yet again, he was wrong.

Chapter Twenty-Five

To Torvil's surprise, the dormitory was exactly as he had known it as a child. There they were, the rows and rows of hand-carved beds, neatly made with sheets and blankets, chalk boards clearly visible in the glow of flickering nightlights. Not that there was any Miss Turi to make notes on them, of course; neither were there any children to make notes about.

Instead, at the far end of the room, with his back to them, sitting on a wooden chair by the stove, was an old man. He was sitting very still, with his head bent forward, and Torvil wondered if he might be asleep. Torvil gave the snowman a meaningful look and, understanding that the elf wished to gain a better vantage point, the giant tiptoed around the edge of the building, dangling Torvil at arm's length.

They approached one of the nearby windows, and now Torvil could see that the old man's head was bent not because he was asleep, but because he was leaning forward, studying what appeared to be an old sepia photograph. Confused, Torvil looked at the snowman and shrugged, but the snowman signalled for him to stay quiet and keep watching. Torvil did as he was told, and turned back just in time to see the old man heave a deep sigh, open the door of the stove, and throw the photograph on to the fire.

For a few seconds the old man watched,

. . . studying what appeared to be an old sepia photograph.

unmoving, as the stiff paper buckled on the hot coals. Then, as if having second thoughts, he snatched a fire iron and swept the picture on to the floor. The edge had come alight, and he immediately smothered the flames with a cushion, taking great care that every last spark was extinguished. He smoothed the blackened paper against his shirt, placed it in his breast pocket, and stood up to walk to the window.

Thinking quickly, the snowman swept Torvil up and retreated to the highway, doing his best impersonation of a snowy hillock. Not that Torvil took much notice; he was too engrossed in the forlorn figure in the window.

As he watched, the old man reached into his pocket and held his palm to the light, as if he was studying some small object. What could it be? Torvil squinted, trying to focus. Then the object flashed silver, and all became clear. It was the

Copper Elf's coin.

Torvil gasped.

'You know who that is now, don't you?' asked the snowman.

'Yes,' said Torvil. 'It's me.'

Chapter Twenty-Six

'Are you all right?' I called out to Father Christmas.

He had broken off from the story and was sitting forward in silence, his right hand loose on the reins, his left hand pinching the bridge of his nose.

For the last few minutes we had been flying over an enormous mangrove swamp at the western tip of Cuba, and the air around us had gone from being very cold and dry to being very warm and moist. I had heard somewhere that rapid changes in temperature could wreak havoc with your nasal membranes, and I wondered if he might be having a nosebleed.

'Shall I put something cold down your back?' I shouted.

'I'm fine,' he said with a slight wobble in his voice, and dabbed his eyes with a large white handkerchief. 'It's just that this story isn't easy to tell.'

For a brief moment, I was confused. Why was he so upset? And then it dawned on me, and all became clear.

'It's you, isn't it?' I asked. 'Torvil is you.'

Father Christmas nodded.

'So that was your future?' I asked. 'Super rich, but super lonely.'

'I came so close,' he said, 'to the most perfect misery.'

For a while we rode in silence, with the wind

whistling, and the sleigh bells clanking. 'What was in the photograph?' I asked.

Father Christmas sighed and reached inside his jacket. 'Here,' he said, handing me a battered leather wallet.

'Open it,' he said.

I've mentioned I'm good at remembering things, but a boy with the memory of a shellfish would never forget the things that were inside that wallet, they were so unexpected. To begin with, there was no money, just leaves.

'What are these for?' I asked.

'What do you mean, what are they for?' replied the elf. 'They're leaves; they're the things that keep trees alive.'

'Yes. But what are they doing in your wallet?'

'So I don't lose them,' came the reply.

And that wasn't all. There was a laminated pilot's licence, issued by the North Pole Aviation

Authority, embossed with his photo; a Nice List written in curly handwriting; a Naughty List in capital letters; a faded map of the world; and an invitation to a brandy tasting from someone called Chivas Regal. And finally, tucked in a corner, was a small square of shiny paper.

Its worn-out folds revealed an ancient sepia photograph of an elf boy and an elf girl, standing side by side next to a Christmas tree. The girl held a toy hedgehog, and I knew straightaway that it must be Gerda. That meant the boy had to be Torvil or, as I now knew him, Father Christmas.

I had so many questions I wanted to ask, but I stayed silent, hoping Father Christmas would keep telling his story.

'You'll remember,' said Father Christmas after a long pause, 'that I ran away from the orphanage, and went travelling the world?'

'Because of Gerda,' I said. 'You were jealous that the butcher's wife adopted her and not you.'

'Yes,' said Father Christmas, 'But over the years, as I was travelling, I realised that it was wrong of me to try and make her choose between me and her new family. The thing about travelling, as you may one day discover, is that the first thing you unpack is yourself.' Father Christmas turned in his seat, so that he could look me in the eye. 'After a few years of seeing the world – and I mean the entire world – my heart softened and I started to miss home. I knew that one day, when I had seen all that I needed to see, I would go back and ask Gerda to forgive me.

'So I decided to do something special for

Gerda, to say sorry and remind her of the friends we had once been. Thinking of the rag toys that Miss Turi had made us, I began to collect the most incredible toys I could find, one for each Christmas we had been apart. In Russia, I bought her the most beautiful set of Matryoshka dolls.'

'What are they?' I asked.

'Oh! They're beautiful,' said Father Christmas. 'Some people call them Russian nesting dolls. They're brightly painted wooden dolls and every time you pull one apart you find a smaller one inside, right down to the tiniest doll you could ever imagine.'

'My sisters would like those,' I said.

'Interesting,' said Father Christmas, and winked. 'Then, in Hungary, I bought her a Rubik's Cube—'

'I love Rubik's Cubes!' I said.

'Duly noted,' said Father Christmas. 'In Togo,

I found an Awale set . . . do you know what that is?'

'No, but it sounds fantastic,' I said.

'You'd love it,' said Father Christmas. 'It's a counting game. In Kenya, a wire car – you have to see one to believe it, they make them so beautifully out of twisted wire. In the Netherlands, I got her a shuffleboard. In the UK, a game called Tiddlywinks—'

'I've got that,' I said.

'So you have,' said Father Christmas, thinking back. 'The same year I got you *The Observer's Book of Birds.*'

'And the red fighter plane whose wheel came off,' I said.

'Really? It had a faulty wheel?' asked Father Christmas, suddenly business-like.

'I'm afraid so,' I said.

'Hmmm, I'll have to look into that,' said

Father Christmas. 'Can't let the standards slip
. . . Anyway, everywhere I went I found Gerda
the most incredible presents. Yahtzee from the
United States, Jumping Caps from Poland, a
bamboo horse from China. And nine Christmases
later, I'd seen enough and I travelled back to the
town. Of course, I was nervous about seeing
Gerda, because we had argued before I left, and
I wasn't sure if she would have forgiven me. So I
stopped off in the tavern for some mead to give
myself some courage.

'I had friends in those days – other children
from the orphanage, mainly – and they had
missed me, and were pleased that I had returned.
I decided to show them the presents I had saved
for Gerda, so I placed them all on the bar. I was
so proud of what I'd bought.

'While we were there, Grimm Grimmsson
came in, the owner of the shoe factory. His

head for business was legendary, and I had admired him ever since I was a boy. This was in the days before he went bust and made off with everyone's wages. He had been too busy working to buy presents for his daughters, and when he saw Gerda's presents he offered to buy them from me.

'Of course, I refused. I had bought the toys for Gerda and I hoped it would mean a lot to her that I'd thought of her while I was away. But Grimm was insistent. He turned his purse upside down on the bar top and out spilled hundreds of bright gold crowns. I had never seen so much money in all my life.

'"Don't be silly," said Grimm. "With the money I'll pay, you can start your own toyshop. Think of all the toys you'll be able to give Gerda then."

'Like a fool, I agreed. When I woke up in

Out spilled hundreds of bright gold crowns.

the morning, I knew straightaway I had made a terrible mistake. As I opened the shutters, I saw Gerda walking down the path to my house. She had heard that I'd returned, and of course she wanted to see me. But I was so ashamed I had sold her presents that I hid and didn't answer the door.

'I kept avoiding her,' said Father Christmas. 'Instead, I used the money to buy my toyshop. The money in my till started to take the place of Gerda, and I began to forget her. I decided that I could never really have cared for her in the first place, that I was better off alone. As time went on I needed more and more money to feel even the tiniest bit happy. It didn't matter how much I earned, it was never enough.'

'So we must be coming to the part of the story where you change,' I said. 'Because you're not mean like that at all! You're one of the most generous people in the whole world.'

'Thank you,' said Father Christmas. 'It's nice to be appreciated. And you're right, of course. We've reached the really crucial part of the story. *Yah!*' he cried to the reindeer, and then straightaway, 'Sorry!'

Rudolph and the other reindeer slowed their gallop and we began to descend. For the last few minutes we had been flying across the Gulf of Mexico; to our right, the lights of Florida stretched out into the dark ocean like the fin of a golden turtle. Next stop would be Miami.

'Where shall we pick it up?' asked Father Christmas.

'Where we left off,' I said. 'You've just seen yourself in the future, all alone.'

'Good idea,' said Father Christmas. 'In which case this, well, this is what happened next . . .'

Chapter Twenty-Seven

No sooner had Torvil realised that the old man at the window must be him than – you guessed it – a sharp gust of wind whipped up the snow, forcing him to raise both arms in front of his face for protection. The gust quickly strengthened to a gale, but just as it seemed fit to blow him over, it suddenly raced upwards, the snow settled, and the world around him fell eerily still and silent.

Glancing up, Torvil saw a very curious thing: up and up went the gust of wind, spiralling round and round the snowman, causing a sudden puff of snow round about its tummy; then another somewhere in the region of its elbow; then finally the snowman's enormous black top hat blew clean off, and circled in the sky above them, like an eagle riding a thermal.

If Torvil had known anything about tornadoes, he might have worried at seeing such a sight; but tornadoes are almost unknown in the North Pole, especially in winter. Little did he know, but that sharp gust of wind had been the first breath of a newborn tornado, and he and the snowman were now standing at its very centre, the place we call the eye of the storm.

The first sign that anything was really wrong came when the snowman decided to reach out to try and re-capture its hat, which was still circling way above its head. As it did so, its hand was blown off, and a long trail of snow began to spiral out from its wrist, up into the sky above them, looking for all the world as if the creature was unfurling a giant streamer.

'Stop!' called Torvil. 'We're surrounded! Don't move!'

But the snowman took no notice. As the hat took wing, it decided to give chase.

As each and every part of the giant creature's body made contact with the tornado, it was blown to smithereens. The enormous wall of wind that surrounded them was suddenly bleached thick with snow, and Torvil saw to his horror that he was trapped in a gigantic swirling funnel of ice that surrounded him on every side, yawning right up into the heavens.

Torvil's feet left the ground, as strange winds swung him like a puppet in an ever-widening spiral, higher and higher. Soon he joined the snowman's top hat, circling round and round,

Strange winds swung him like a puppet.

hundreds of metres above the ground; shortly after that he glimpsed the Copper Elf, clutching his sack-pipe. Old Miss Turi flew past, her skirt billowing; next came the reindeer, sneezing violently. He saw the fir tree dancing a jig, and Steinar the Elf and his family clinging to their tiny dinner table. Finally, he came face to face with Gerda, who reached out her hands for Torvil to take hold.

'Wake up, Torvil!' called Gerda, her voice drowned by the winds. 'Wake up!'

Chapter Twenty-Eight

Torvil opened his eyes to find himself sitting upright in low fog, his back slumped against the orphanage gates.

'Wake up!' said the sleigh driver, taking him by the hands and pulling him to his feet. 'Wake up!'

'Where am I?' asked Torvil. 'Is this heaven?'

'Not quite,' said the sleigh driver. 'It's a bus stop. It was me dropped you here, sir, about an hour ago, on my way into town. Now I'm on my way back. Come on, let's get you home.'

'Wait, wait . . . erm,' said Torvil, coming to his senses. 'I'm so sorry – I don't know your name.'

'That's because you've never asked,' said the sleigh driver.

'For which I am truly sorry,' said Torvil. 'Can you find it in your heart to forgive me?'

'Err . . . yes,' said the driver, unsure what had brought about such a marked change in his most miserable passenger. 'Yes, I suppose I can. My name is Erik.'

'Erik!' said Torvil. 'Erik!' His eyes filled with tears. 'My name is Torvil. Pleased to meet you, Erik.' And without any warning, he gave Erik the most enormous bear hug.

'Pleased to meet you, Torvil,' said Erik, slightly bemused.

'Erik,' said Torvil, placing a comradely hand on each of Erik's shoulders.

'Yes, Torvil?' said Erik.

'What day is it today?'

Erik shrugged his shoulders. Surely Torvil must know?

'It's Christmas Day.'

'I hoped so. I hoped so! Happy Christmas, Erik!' And with those words, Torvil bounded off into the snow.

'Happy Christmas!' called Erik.

Chapter Twenty-Nine

'Yes, all right!' called Gerda in the darkness, as she struggled to light the old oil lamp in the butcher's shop. 'I'm coming!'

Not that it made much difference. Whoever was outside just kept on knocking, as if they were determined to wake the entire house. Tutting, Gerda took the key from its hook, opened the door, and came face to face with Torvil Christmas.

'Gerda,' he said breathlessly.

'Torvil?' she replied, stunned.

'I'm so sorry,' he said.

'For what?' asked Gerda suspiciously.

'For everything. For being jealous when you were adopted, for arguing with you, for running away, for not speaking to you when I came back. For all of it,' said Torvil.

'Ah, I see,' said Gerda, smiling. 'That's very clever! Let me see . . . I've got something for you here somewhere,' she said, handing him a coin from her pocket. 'That's some pretty impressive shape-changing,' she said. 'Merry Christmas. Now go on, let's see who you really are.'

'Gerda, it's not a magic trick,' said Torvil. 'It really is me.'

'What?' said Gerda.

'I've had the most extraordinary night,' said Torvil, his words tumbling out so fast he could only just manage to get them in the right order.

'One day I'll tell you the whole story, but for now . . . I'm changing my ways.'

'What's going on here?' came a gruff voice from the back of the shop, and Gerda and Torvil turned to see the butcher framed by the doorway.

'It's the toy seller, Father, from across the street,' replied Gerda.

'Is it, indeed?' said the butcher, stepping forward into the lamplight. Torvil could now see that his enormous moustache was covered with a net that hooked up behind his ears. 'The same toy seller I refused as a boy? The same toy seller who has worked opposite me for two hundred and fifty years and never spent so much as a penny in my shop?'

'The same, sir,' said Torvil boldly. 'Though as I was just telling Gerda, I am a changed man, and have more than words to prove it. In fact, I would like to buy your largest goose.'

'*Humph!*' snorted the butcher, deeply unimpressed. 'Would you indeed? Our largest goose! It's Christmas Day, sir, and anyone with a brain in their head booked their bird the day of the first frost. Fetch yourself a good throwing stone and try and knock a robin off its perch. Pluck it, pop a raisin in its bottom and roast it over a lighted match; that's going to be the closest you'll get to Christmas dinner this year.'

'But, Father,' said Gerda, 'we do have one goose left. I plucked it last night.'

'No, no, no,' said the butcher, smiling. 'That's a monster. Heavier than a dining chair. He hasn't the strength to even pick it up. Besides —' and he now sauntered right up to Torvil, drawing himself to his full height — 'it's worth a small fortune, and this one's tighter than a spider's purse.'

Torvil laughed. 'It's true,' he said, his eyes twinkling, 'I've been a miser, a hoarder and a skinflint, and I too can scarcely believe the change in me. But here I am, and more to the point, here is my gold.'

With that, Torvil took a leather drawstring bag from his pocket and handed it to the butcher.

'Take whatever you feel is the right price.'

The butcher frowned. Even without looking inside, he could tell from its weight that the purse was worth a great, great deal.

'Gerda,' said the butcher. 'Fetch the goose.'

Gerda nodded, and did as she was told.

'She doesn't know,' said the butcher quietly, so that only Torvil could hear.

'Doesn't know what?' said Torvil.

'Why you're really here,' said the butcher. 'But I do.' As he spoke, he produced a large leather-bound ledger.

'Do you know what this is?'

'Your accounts?' asked Torvil.

'*Her* accounts,' said the butcher. 'This –' he turned the pages slowly, savouring the hundreds and thousands of tiny handwritten numbers – 'is my right.'

'I don't understand . . .' said Torvil.

'If you think you can just take Gerda away, then you're wrong,' said the butcher. 'If she goes with you, then this –' he stuck out his tongue, while he made a swift calculation – 'this is the reckoning.'

'Two hundred and ninety-three thousand, eight hundred and twenty-five crowns,' read Torvil.

'Well, we agree on something,' said the butcher.

'Firstly,' said Torvil, 'you are an ogre, a beast and a brute, and how you ever came to have the good fortune of adopting Gerda as a daughter I will never understand—'

'She's no daughter of mine,' said the butcher. 'Adopting her was my wife's idea and I've been lumbered with her ever since.'

Once again, Torvil felt a pang of guilt. How had he let Gerda be treated in this way?

'Do not forget, sir,' he said, speaking clear and close, 'that I have seen with my own eyes the comings and goings of this household. Gerda has worked for you, unpaid, since the day she left the orphanage; ever since your poor wife died, she has cared for you as tenderly as any daughter could, cooked your meals, washed your clothes, and tended you when you were sick. Gerda owes you nothing.'

'Let me stop you there,' said the butcher, 'because we need to find you a high horse to sit on.'

'Gerda is the kindest—'

'Kindness doesn't pay my bills,' said the butcher with a smirk.

The words hit Torvil like punch to the stomach, and he took a sharp intake of breath. Had he not once said something similar to the customers in his shop? Had they seen him as he now saw the butcher: a man so obsessed with money that he had lost all feeling?

It was then that he remembered the coin in his pocket.

'Do you know what this is?' said Torvil, pulling out the coin and flashing it between his finger and thumb.

'Where did you get that?' asked the butcher, greedily staring at the silver.

'It was given to me,' said Torvil.

''Course it was,' scoffed the butcher. 'A penny from the First Elves. People just give them away like toffees at the fair.'

'Will this do?' asked Torvil.

'Do for what?' said the butcher.

'Will this free Gerda from her bond?'

'*Humph*,' snorted the butcher again. And then, when Torvil's expression failed to change, 'You mean it?'

'If you'll take it, it's yours,' said Torvil, and placed the coin in the palm of the butcher's hand.

The butcher closed his huge sausage-like fingers around the coin.

'May it keep you as you deserve to be kept,' said Torvil.

That was when Gerda appeared in the doorway, struggling to carry the most enormous goose that Torvil had ever seen.

'Gerda, let me help you,' said Torvil, and the two of them placed the bird in a withy basket,

'May it keep you as you deserve to be kept' said Torvil.

taking a handle each.

'There's no way he can carry this on his own, Father,' said Gerda to the butcher. 'Would you mind awfully if I helped deliver it?'

'You're free to do whatever you choose,' said the butcher, looking Torvil straight in the eye.

'Shall we?' said Torvil, and the two of them began the tricky business of steering the goose through the doorway of the shop and out on to the street.

'Goodbye, Father,' said Gerda to the butcher, and the door sprang shut, ringing the bell.

'Goodbye, girl,' said the butcher.

A cold draught rushed to greet him, and he shivered violently, as if he was being entered by some evil spirit. He opened his fingers. There, resting in the palm of his pink hand, was the beautiful silver elfin penny. Turning the coin over, the butcher could see that on the back were three pictures: a robin, a penguin and a polar bear.

At that very moment, there was a tap on the window, and the butcher looked up to see a robin perched on the ledge. The butcher frowned. The robin tapped the glass with its beak, and gestured with one of its wings. It seemed to want him to come outside.

Chapter Thirty

'Please do come in,' said Torvil, holding open the toyshop door with the heel of his boot, as he and Gerda struggled with either end of the colossal goose. 'We'll set it down on the counter while I light the kiln.'

'Kiln?' said Gerda.

'The shop doesn't have an oven,' said Torvil. 'But we do have a kiln. I'll get it nice and hot and we'll have this goose roasted by lunchtime.'

'Not without some herbs, you won't,' said Gerda. 'Where's your kitchen?'

'I don't really have one,' said Torvil sheepishly. 'I don't allow lunchbreaks in the shop … or, at least, I didn't. I probably will now. I mean, I *definitely* will.'

'In that case,' said Gerda, 'I am going to knock on doors until I find some. I can't have you eating your Christmas dinner with an unseasoned goose, it just wouldn't be right.'

'Actually the goose isn't for me,' said Torvil. 'It's for my … someone I work with.'

'Well, then,' said Gerda, smiling and heading for the door, 'I'm going to hunt down an orange as well. Goose tastes wonderful with orange.'

With Gerda gone, Torvil was alone in the shop for a few moments and he felt a strange warm feeling in his heart that had been absent for so long. His chin rose and his shoulders dropped. He was finding himself again, remembering the elf he had once been.

He looked around the shop, but instead of

feeling his usual burst of pride and excitement at all the money he could make from the toys he felt sad. Sad that so many beautiful toys were sitting lonely on the shelf, while so many of the town's children would be without presents on Christmas Day. And guilty at the prices – newly doubled with nothing but profit in mind.

His eye fell on a beautiful red bicycle. And in that very moment, an extraordinary thought came to him; a thought that would change the world.

Seconds later, when Gerda returned with a basket full of salt, pepper, butter, oranges and fresh herbs that she had begged and borrowed from her friends and neighbours, she found Torvil standing in the middle of the toyshop, beaming from ear to ear.

'Gerda!' he cried, his eyes full of tears. 'I know what we have to do. We have to give the toys away!'

Chapter Thirty-One

'Come on!' cried Torvil, picking up a wooden train set from the shelf and balancing a toy aeroplane on top of it. 'We are going to make sure that every child in this town has a fabulous Christmas. Quick, pass me that doll's house!'

'Torvil?' said Gerda. 'Are you sure you feel quite well?'

'Yes,' said Torvil. 'I've never been better.'

'But Torvil . . .' said Gerda. 'You can't just give your toys away.'

'That's just it!' said Torvil. 'I can and I will!'

And, with that, he rushed outside, without stopping even to button up his jacket. Shaking her head, Gerda picked up the doll's house and joined him in the street.

'Excuse me, sir!' said Torvil.

A Mining Elf was passing, carrying a pickaxe, his face black with coal dust.

'Sir, do you have any children?' Torvil asked.

'Yes!' said the Mining Elf, hoisting the pickaxe off his shoulder so that he could rest it on the ground. 'I've got nine. What's it to you?'

'Would they like these toys?' asked Torvil.

The elf looked at the toys, then looked at Torvil. 'Why?' he asked, with suspicion. 'What's wrong with them?'

'Nothing,' said Torvil.

'Then why are you giving them away?' said the Mining Elf.

'Because it's Christmas!'

The Mining Elf stared at Torvil. Then he smiled. And then he burst into hysterical laughter. 'Very good!' he said. 'Very good. You don't give anything away for free! Well, you're not tricking me into taking faulty toys! Good day to you!' He hoisted his pickaxe back on to his shoulder, and continued on his way.

Torvil rejoined Gerda on the other side of the road.

'What happened?' said Gerda.

'He wouldn't take them,' said Torvil. 'I think he thought it was some kind of trick. People don't trust me.'

'Let me try,' said Gerda. She crossed the street to a neighbouring house and, balancing the toys as best she could on one arm, she knocked at the door. There was no reply, so she knocked again. One of the upstairs lights came on, and a few moments later an elf woman wearing a large felt hat appeared in the doorway. Gerda showed her the toys, and – just as with the Mining Elf – the woman shook her head and closed the door. Gerda made her way back across the empty street.

'And?' said Torvil.

'She couldn't believe that that you would be giving toys away,' said Gerda.

'This is terrible,' said Torvil. 'We have to give the children their toys.'

'If only we could get inside somehow and just leave them to be found,' said Gerda.

'Oh, if only!' exclaimed Torvil. 'But all their doors are locked. The only way in is down the—'

He stopped abruptly and looked at Gerda.

'Chimney?' she asked.

'But how would I fit the toys in?'

Gerda smiled. 'Oh, I don't know,' she said. 'What about your magic delivery sack?'

Bit by bit, a broad smile began to spread across Torvil's face.

'We couldn't,' he said. 'Could we?'

Chapter Thirty-Two

Torvil ran his finger around the inside edge of the chimney pot, and held it up for closer inspection. It was covered in soot.

'Torvil!' hissed Gerda from the alley below. 'Hurry up!' After a few wrong turnings, Torvil had managed to locate Steinar's cottage, tucked away in the East Village. He was now up on the roof, while Gerda stood guard.

'Are you sure there's no other way in?' asked Torvil, in as loud a voice as he dared.

Torvil ran his finger around the inside edge of the chimney pot.

'Positive!' called Gerda. 'The door's locked,' she said, testing it again just to make sure. 'And so are all the windows.'

'Good. Good,' said Torvil. 'Then this is definitely the way forward,' he said, thinking to himself that it definitely wasn't. He was about to tell Gerda that he thought he might be allergic to coal dust, when his eye caught something peeping out from the sack of toys beside him: the front wheel of the red bicycle. And then it hit him: if he didn't go through with this, then Kiti wouldn't get a bicycle for Christmas, and no matter how little he liked the thought of climbing down the inside of a filthy chimney, that just couldn't be right.

'Okay,' he hissed. 'I'm going in.'

Taking a deep breath, he swung his right leg over the edge of the chimney pot, then his left. Once he had a toe-hold, he gathered up the toy sack and swung it over his shoulder.

He was now crouching inside the chimney pot, with just his head peeping out.

'Okay, I'm going to slowly make my way down,' he called to Gerda, which was the last thing she heard him say before he fell.

Gerda rushed to the window, where she saw a huge cloud of ash billow out from the fireplace. When it settled, there was Torvil, his red velvet coat and hat completely covered in soot. Gerda had to put her hand over her mouth so that he didn't see her laughing. Thankfully, Torvil was coughing so much he didn't notice. Once he had recovered his composure, Gerda gestured for him to open the window.

'Right,' said Torvil opening up the sack. 'Where shall I leave the bicycle?'

'By the tree,' said Gerda. 'That way Kiti will know it's for Christmas.'

'Good idea,' said Torvil, and went to do as he was told. Seconds later, he was back.

'What about the small stuff?' he said.

'Leave that by the tree too,' said Gerda.

'But we want Kiti to know they are presents,' said Torvil. 'She might think they are decorations. You know, that have fallen off.'

'I know!' said Gerda excitedly. 'Take off one of your stockings.'

'Why?' said Torvil.

'Just do it,' said Gerda. 'Quick.'

Shaking his head, Torvil pulled off one of his boots, then peeled off one of his red woollen socks.

'Put all the little toys in that,' said Gerda, 'and put them at the bottom of Kiti's bed.'

'Are you serious?' said Torvil. 'What if she wakes up?'

'She won't,' said Gerda. 'Not if you are really,

really quiet.'

'Right,' said Torvil, and quickly filled the stocking with lots of small presents. He was just about to tiptoe up the stairs when he stopped, remembering something. He went over to his sack of toys, and rummaged about in the bottom of it. Finally, he found it: an orange. Carefully, he slipped the orange into the toe of the sock.

'Why the orange?' asked Gerda.

'I have no idea,' said Torvil.

Seconds later, Torvil let himself out of the front door, and joined Gerda in the alleyway. He was beaming from ear to ear. 'We did it, Gerda!' he said joyfully. 'We did it!'

'We've done one tiny part of it,' said Gerda. 'What about all the other children? I mean, look at all these houses! How are we going to get round all of them before everyone wakes up?

Torvil's heart sank. Gerda was right. It had

taken for ever to climb up on to Steinar's roof, and this was one of the smallest houses in the town, and therefore one of the easiest to climb. How was he going to get round all the others?

It was then that they heard a loud sniffle from behind them in the alley. Torvil and Gerda turned to see a large reindeer with a runny-looking nose.

'Can I be of any assistance?' said a familiar voice.

'Rudolph!' exclaimed Torvil. 'You're real!'

'As real as it gets,' said Rudolph.

And without a further word between them, Torvil swung himself up on to the reindeer's back, settled his bag of toys over his shoulder, and took off into the night.

Chapter Thirty-Three

When Torvil and Gerda arrived at Steinar's house with the roast goose, of course they didn't say anything about the visit they had made earlier that morning while everyone was asleep.

'Special delivery,' said Torvil with a smile, when Steinar opened the door. 'Righto,' said Steinar, 'I'll grab my coat.'

'No, wait,' said Torvil, holding up a large serving plate, covered with a giant silver cloche. 'This is nothing to do with work. This is for you.'

'And so are these,' said Gerda, peeping out from behind a tower of steaming serving dishes.

'I'm sorry,' said Steinar, 'I really don't understand . . .'

'You've put food on my table all year,' said Torvil, humbly, 'with your beautiful toys. Now I'd like to return the favour. Please?'

He stepped forward and placed the goose in Steinar's hands.

'You've brought me Christmas dinner?' asked Steinar.

'The very least I could do,' said Torvil.

There was a pause, while Steinar looked at the goose, then at Torvil and Gerda, trying to make sense of it all.

'I'm sorry,' he said finally. 'I can't accept this.' Torvil's face fell. 'Unless . . .'

'Unless what?' asked Torvil.

'Unless you both agree to join us,' said Steinar, breaking into a smile.

'We'd love to,' said Gerda.

Within minutes, the table was set and the company seated. With a flourish, Steinar removed the cloche to reveal the goose, golden brown and stuffed to bursting with oranges, chestnuts, sage and thyme; the dish around it was spilling over with bitter sprouts, sweet carrots, succulent cabbage and crispy roast potatoes. There was no fit reaction other than applause, and Gerda bobbed a curtsy.

But the true delights of a Christmas dinner, as you will know, are the trimmings, and Gerda had spared no detail. Every corner of the table was sentried with tall jars of chutney, compote, coulis, mustard and relish; and a flotilla of china jugs began to make their way up and down the table, laden with steaming bread sauces, rich-smelling port gravies and eye-wateringly sweet-and-sour cranberry jams.

Jokes were told, backs were slapped, eyelashes were batted, and long and tedious stories related with unforgivable attention to detail. With every mouthful, the room became cosier, and hearts became closer. Finally chairs were pushed back, pipes lit, and a huge log laid carefully on the fire. It was then that they noticed that the ceiling was awash with blue light. The blue moment had arrived, and day had finally triumphed over night. The door and shutters were opened, and the four adults watched with broad smiles as Kiti rode up and down the tiny alleyway on her brand new red bicycle.

Chapter Thirty-Four

'And that,' whispered the elf, 'is how I became Father Christmas. Doubly so, because shortly afterwards I married Gerda, and she gave birth to my nine sons.'

We were on the top floor of a brownstone in Brooklyn, New York City, getting ready to deliver presents for three children called Ethan, Caleb and Madison. Over the past few minutes we had visited thirty-seven states, and delivered 47.2 million presents.

'You married Gerda!' I said. 'I'm so glad. So

she's Mrs Christmas?'

'One and the same,' said the elf.

Maybe you've heard of the magic key? Until that night, I hadn't, and I had always wondered how Father Christmas manages to get into houses where they don't have chimneys. Well, it turns out that he has a special key, made by the elves, which fits any lock. I did ask him why he still bothered climbing down chimneys if he could just come straight in through the door, and I have to say, I thought his answer was very interesting indeed.

'I like chimneys,' he said simply. 'They're fast and they get you right where you need to be. Like a fireman's pole. Yes, a fireman could walk down the stairs to get to the fire engine, but it's the pole that will get him there quickest. Plus –' he paused and turned to look at me – 'chimneys keep it real. Remind me of where I started.'

The magic key, which had been feeling its way around the inside of the lock, suddenly took a grip of the mechanism and pulled back the bolt on the door. Father Christmas looked at me, triumphant, then carefully pushed back the door so that he could see inside.

'Clear,' he said. 'Let's go.'

We crept down the hallway, searching each room for the Christmas tree. Eventually I spotted it in the kitchen.

I set Father Christmas down, and we began checking the labels at the top of the sack. After a night of rummaging for presents, I'd realised that the sack wasn't just magic because it could hold so many toys, but because the presents you were looking for would somehow always rise to the top.

'But wait,' I whispered. 'I know you started with elves. But why did you start giving presents to humans?'

'Ah,' said Father Christmas. 'That came with the factory.'

'Factory?' I asked, placing what could only be a football under the tree.

'I couldn't go on charging top whack, so I decided to drop my prices. Amazingly, I started to sell more toys than ever. Soon Steinar couldn't keep up with demand, so we took over the old shoe factory, and employed all the out-of-work elves as toymakers,' said Father Christmas. In the time it had taken me to lay one present, he had set out all the rest. There they were in three neat piles, one for each child. 'Luckily, all the skills involved in shoemaking – leather work, stitching, hammering – are very useful in toymaking,' he continued. 'So, if an elf can make a great pair of shoes, he or she can also make a great My Little Pony, or a Gravity Maze.'

'So all the elves had jobs again?'

'Exactly,' said Father Christmas. We were now in the hallway, where he closed the door, and tested the handle, just to make sure we hadn't left it unlocked. 'And, just as they had once bought elfin shoes, humans started to buy elfin toys. You must have noticed that feeling of magic when you enter a human toyshop?' He peered at me over his little round glasses. 'It's because all the toys are made by elves.'

'I never knew that,' I said, and carried him back out into the street.

'All the good ones, anyway. And if humans buy our toys throughout the year – for birthdays and so on – then it's only fair that we give them free toys at Christmas.'

'How's your ankle?' I asked.

'The swelling's gone down,' said Father Christmas. 'Thanks to you. I reckon I'll be able to put weight on it soon.'

We were now back at the sleigh, and I lifted him up into the driver's seat.

'Do you want to know the real secret?' he asked. 'The thing I discovered that very first Christmas?'

'Yes, please,' I said, as I climbed up beside him.

'It's lovely to receive a present. But the good feeling fades after a while, and you just find you want something else. When you give something . . . and you don't tell anyone . . . well, that good feeling stays with you for ever.'

With that, he shook the reins and the reindeer began to gather pace. The snow was patchy on the ground, and the sleigh's rails sparked every time they met the tarmac. We turned a corner, and suddenly right in front of us was the Manhattan Bridge. I was just beginning to wonder how we were ever going to clear it when Rudolph made a glorious leap up into the moonlight, and we went rushing towards the stars.

Chapter Thirty-Five

At least, I think that's what happened. The truth is, by then I was beginning to feel very sleepy indeed. I remember flying over the Niagara Falls, with Lake Eerie and Lake Ontario stretched out on either side, but I must have fallen asleep, because I can't remember any more of the journey.

Meanwhile, Father Christmas must have carried on his deliveries, visiting Vermont, then New Hampshire and Maine, before crossing the Canadian border to New Brunswick and Nova

Scotia, looping back via Prince Edward Island and Newfoundland, sweeping up to Quebec and Ontario and zig-zagging west from Manitoba to the Nunavut to Saskatchewan to the Northwest Territories to Alberta, then daisy-chaining through British Colombia and the Yukon to mop up Alaska.

And then, having finished all of his North American deliveries, he must have swooped across the globe to return to my house to drop me off.

But, really, I'm just guessing . . .

Because the only thing I remember was waking up in my fireplace, covered in soot. I felt something moving underneath me, and it was a few seconds before I realised it was Father Christmas. Despite being only half my height, he had somehow managed to carry me from the sleigh to the chimney pot, and was now face down in the cold ashes.

Suddenly wide awake, I jumped up and helped him to his feet. 'Are you all right?' I asked with concern.

'I think I've twisted my ankle again,' he said. 'It had only just started feeling better.'

'Here, take a seat,' I said.

'Is there any brandy?' he asked hopefully.

'Um, I think you drank it all before we left,' I said. 'But don't worry, I'll fetch you another bag of frozen peas.'

'Whoop-ee-doo,' he said.

When I returned from the kitchen, he had a grave look on his face.

'Look, I'm sorry about this,' he said. 'But I am going to need one last bit of help. These are for you and your sisters,' he said, handing me his sack of presents.

'I'd be delighted,' I replied, sweeping the bag

'I am going to need one last bit of help.'

up onto my shoulder.

'And, Jackson . . .'

'Yes?' I asked.

'Thank you.'

I smiled. I somehow knew that when I came back downstairs, he wouldn't be there, and that this was us saying goodbye.

'Merry Christmas, Jackson' he said.

'Merry Christmas, Father Christmas,' I replied.

That night I had delivered millions of presents, but Father Christmas had always been with me. Now, as I climbed the stairs with the world-famous sack in my hands, I really felt the pressure. My sisters were depending on me, and I mustn't let them down.

Hardly daring to breathe, I crept into their room. There, at the end of their beds, were their empty stockings. I couldn't really see in the dark, so I just trusted the sack to hand me the right presents. I knew if I made a sound — any sound at all — my sisters would wake up and see me, and then they would never believe in Father Christmas ever again.

Once I was done, I crept silently down the hall, and placed Father Christmas's sack at the bottom of my bed. He and I had delivered presents to all the children in the world, except one. Whatever was left, I reasoned to myself, must be meant for me.

So it was still a surprise when I woke the next morning, and delved into the bottom of the sack. Most years I got some of the things on my list, but this year . . . well, I got every single thing that I wanted. Even the exact Star Wars Han Solo action figure I had asked for. There was a present I hadn't asked for too, but always secretly wanted: a telescope for looking at the stars. That's the really cool thing about Father Christmas – he knows you better than you know yourself.

My sisters had a great Christmas too. As well as the Duplo set and the Nerf guns they had both asked for, there were two of the most beautiful Matryoshka dolls. To begin with, neither of them knew what they were. But I was able to explain and to do some great big brother work by showing them how each one came apart in the middle, and inside was another, slightly smaller doll, and how you could set them all out so you had a whole row. That's a bit like people.

Inside us is every person we've ever been, even from when we were very small.

They loved the dolls so much, at one point I very nearly told my sisters it was me who had laid their presents out, not Father Christmas. But then I remembered what he had told me: when you give something, and you don't tell anyone, the good feeling stays with you for ever. So I stayed quiet.

I felt so bad for tricking my mother and father the night before that when they came downstairs, the first thing I did was to give them both a big hug, even though I didn't usually like that kind of thing because it made my skin itch. Once my sisters had shown them their presents, which by that point were mostly broken, I saw them go over to check the tray we'd left for Father Christmas by the fire.

'Look, Jackson. The mince pie's gone,' said

my mother.

'And the brandy,' added my father.

Sure enough, there were the crumbs from the mince pie, an empty brandy glass, and a missing carrot. I didn't tell them about my adventure with Father Christmas, because I wasn't sure that they'd believe me. But looking at the evidence, I knew it had to be true.

Acknowledgements

The first person I wish to thank is my super-talented wife Jessica Parker, who strongly encouraged me to begin a Christmas story. And the second is my super-dynamic agent Luigi Bonomi, who strongly encouraged me to finish it. Daniela Terrazzini is a phenomenal illustrator, and it has been a joy to see her bring these characters to life, while casting her own magic spell over the entire book. My sublimely gifted friends Ruth Jones, Alexander Armstrong, and Philip Ardagh were kind enough to read early drafts, and even kinder to supply incendiary quotes. And thanks also to the inimitable (trust me, I've tried, and it's impossible) Charles Dickens, who made some of the early running with *A Christmas Carol*.

I am blessed with a brilliant editor in Jane Griffiths. It was love at first re-write, and I am deeply grateful to her and the rest of the superlative Alex Maramenides' s crack team at Simon & Schuster for nurturing this book so protectively and believing in it so completely: to Jenny Richards for the stunning design; Sarah Macmillan, Eve Wersocki Morris, and Jade Westwood for their imaginative marketing and PR (and for building me my very own grotto); to Jenny Glencross and Leena Lane for their elevating copyedits; to Jane Pizzey for her forensic proofread; to Laura Hough and the Sales team for their judicious matchmaking with only the most eligible of retail partners; and to Sophie Marchbank for her seamless and painstaking production.

Thanks also to my luminously brilliant acting agent Samira Davies, and her equally luminous and equally brilliant assistants Lisa Stretton and Geri Spicer at Independent; you have been more than patient, in fact you have been supportive from the get-go. And nothing would ever have got done without my unquestionably rockstar personal assistant, Tasha Brade.

But no Christmas story would ever get out of the blocks without the selfless dedication of one man in particular. Or to be more accurate, one *elf* in particular. Father Christmas, we thank you. Long may you rein. Come on, everyone's allowed one pun.